Dangerous Secrets

By Lisa Renee Jones
Copyright 2012

Book 2 of the New York Times Best Selling TALL,
DARK, and DEADLY.

Includes an excerpt from *If I Were You* -
From the INSIDE OUT series now OPTIONED
TO STARZ FOR TV with Suzanne Todd (Alice in
Wonderland w/Johnny Depp) producing.

The Tall, Dark, and Deadly series includes:

Book 1: Hot Secrets - Out Now
Book 2: Dangerous Secrets - Out Now

Also available

Book 3: Beneath the Secrets - Out Now

www.lisareneejones.com.

The Walker Brothers...

Tall, dark, and deadly, these three brothers run Walker Security. Each brother is unique in his methods and skills, but all share key similarities. They are passionate about those they love, relentless when fighting for a cause they believe in, and all believe that no case is too hard, no danger too dark. Dedication is what they deliver, results are their reward.

Get Walker Brother wallpaper at

www.lisareneejones.com

"Greed is a stronger force than gravity."

Chapter One

He has nasty little habits," Elizabeth Moore said with a dramatic pause before adding, "both in and out of the bedroom. Things people wouldn't expect from a judge."

Julie Harrison fixed her client's soon to be ex-wife in an unblinking stare from across her desk, intentionally showing no reaction. "Mrs. Moore, you really shouldn't be here. I'm not trying to be insensitive, but I represent your husband in this divorce and I'm bound by certain laws and preset boundaries that I simply don't have the liberty to ignore."

"I'm not surprised he chose you as his attorney," she replied pointedly. "He has a thing for blondes, you know." Her gaze crudely raked Julie's rather voluptuous figure.

There was a silent 'bimbo' inference, and it grated on Julie's nerves, reminding her a little too much of her Vegas showgirl mother and four stepfathers. She'd heard a lot of those inferences in law school, and they'd hurt, but they'd also motivated her to work hard and prove herself. She accepted that she'd never have the Audrey Hepburn elegance that Elizabeth Moore personified years before. Mostly. Once in a blue moon though, she still burned for the instant respect a woman like Mrs. Moore claimed when she entered a room, rather than, well, whatever it was Julie herself evoked in people.

"As I've said, Mrs. Moore," Julie pressed, trying to direct their conversation to an end, "I think it would be best if you have your attorney contact me. I shouldn't have agreed to see you. When you said this was a matter of life and death, I was concerned for everyone's safety."

"I believe you'll understand what I meant when I finish explaining why I'm here." Mrs. Moore leaned back in her chair and crossed her legs. "I'm also certain you'll agree it's best kept between the two of us. See, I'm prepared to make my husband's nasty little habits public if that's what it takes to get a fair shake in this divorce."

Alarm bells went off at the shockingly blatant threat, especially considering Elizabeth's reputation as a charming woman involved in a variety of charitable organizations. Nothing about this visit fit that reputation, but, much to Julie's disapproval, Judge Moore had cut off all his wife's credit cards and cash flow. Not only was Elizabeth Moore in a bad position, but her actions drove home that desperation was never smart nor pretty.

"Threatening a sex scandal seems a bit beneath you," Julie warned softly, hating to see what the judge was bringing out in her, trying to bring her back to reason.

Elizabeth let out a humorless laugh. "Oh, honey, his sexual preferences might be kinky, but they are nothing compared to some of his other, shall we say, addictions."

Her words lingered in the air for several silent moments, inviting scary prospects to run through Julie's mind. Against her better judgment, she said, "I'm listening."

A look of triumph settled on Elizabeth's face. "As you well know, he's an art collector. He doesn't make all of his pieces public. Some of it is kept underground." She paused for obvious effect. "In a hidden vault." A slow smile turned up the corners of Elizabeth's delicate mouth. "There are people who would be very interested in some of the items my husband has in his keeping. It could cause him quite a bit of trouble."

"What exactly are you saying?" Julie asked, afraid of what the answer was going to be. Pornography, or worse even, child pornography? Please say it isn't so, she thought.

Elizabeth pushed to her feet. "Tell him two can play dirty. It's best you know nothing more because, while I don't like you, Ms. Harrison, I don't want you to end up dead." With that she turned and headed toward the door.

"Elizabeth," Julie called out, not wanting to seem too anxious as she barely kept herself in her seat.

Elizabeth turned. "Yes?"

"If it's that dangerous for me to know whatever this secret is, aren't you putting yourself in danger by issuing this threat?"

"My husband won't kill me," she said. "He won't kill you, either. But there are others who'll kill us all if they find out what he's hiding. He won't expect this from me. I've been weak where he's concerned. Now that I've proven I'm not, he won't risk me taking this further. He'll give me what I want." She gave a nod. "Goodbye, Ms. Harrison."

Julie watched her leave, stunned by just how nasty this had gotten, then rotated her chair to take in the view from her fifteenth floor downtown Manhattan window. "What in the heck just happened?" she mumbled to the empty room. And why oh why did it have to happen now? Tomorrow, she would leave for Chicago to negotiate the divorce settlement for one of her many professional athlete clients. A few days later, her best friend, Lauren Reynolds, was getting married, and she was maid of honor. Complications were not well-timed.

Sighing, she punched the button on her intercom. "Gina," she said, calling her assistant for the past six months. "Can you please track down Judge Moore?"

"Of course," Gina said promptly. She was always prompt. Prickly but efficient, and that was what mattered.

Julie reached for her coffee cup, and while she wasn't usually a drinker, she wished she had some hard stuff right now. At nine o'clock in the morning she was wishing for alcohol. What did that say about her life? She didn't know what was wrong with her lately, but she had this sense of dissatisfaction that belied the growing high profile client list that should have her reveling in her success. Maybe she should consider joining the small firm Lauren had left the District Attorney's office for. The firm she was with wasn't a powerhouse, but it wasn't an ant farm either. Still, she was nearly thirty now, and had to think about her future. After seven years here, she couldn't say they'd helped her career. She'd been hired to handle corporate law, but they'd thrown her divorce cases no one had wanted and she'd made it work.

Her intercom buzzed. "The judge is on two."

"Got it," Julie said, punching the button before lifting the receiver to her ear. "Judge?"

He made an irritated noise. "I'm heading into court, Julie. What's so important it couldn't wait?"

Julie bit back the retort that threatened to slip out, managing an unaffected voice. "Your wife stopped by."

"Oh, well hell," he grumbled. "Surely this can wait."

"I don't know, Judge, you tell me. She seems to think she has some information you don't want leaked. Her exact words were 'I can play dirty too'."

There was a pregnant silence.

"Go on," he said a little too quietly.

Intentionally vague, Julie said, "She mentioned artwork."

Silence, thick, and full of implications filtered through the phone line.

He cleared his throat. "Exactly what did she say about the subject?"

Not good, Julie thought. "She seems to think you have some pieces you don't want anyone to know about," Julie offered in a neutral tone as she tapped her pencil on her oak desktop.

"Such as?" he asked a pinch of urgency slipping into his tone.

"She wouldn't say," Julie told him in a voice that was deceptively light. "Seemed to think I was better off not knowing."

Silence again. He was having a quiet panic attack, Julie realized with concern.

He cleared his throat again. Julie waited; still nothing. "Judge?"

"It's not a problem," he assured her in a very tight voice. "There are thieves who will go to great lengths to get their hands on highly sought after art. I am always quite nervous about some of my holdings becoming targets. I will have the pieces in question put somewhere safe. Give me forty-eight hours, and then call her bluff."

"It's not a bluff if you think she'll act on it," Julie argued. "And if you need forty-eight hours, that tells me you think she might. Judge, I don't want to offend you, but," she paused to consider her phrasing and decided to be direct. "I need to be sure there is nothing going on I wouldn't want to be involved with."

He laughed, but it sounded forced. "I'm a judge for God's sake. Give me some credit. I have masterpieces that certain collectors would literally kill for. I don't want those pieces of my collection made public. Now do as I say, and call her bluff."

Bluff. There was that word again that sat all kinds of wrong in her mind. "All right, Judge. Consider it done."

Julie's stomach churned with a sense of dread. Nothing about this situation was done. Her gut said that this was going someplace very bad, very quickly.

Chicago O' Hare Airport
Wednesday night, two days later

Ten minutes. That was all Julie had to get to her gate and board. Considering the snowstorm blasting across the state, she couldn't afford to miss it, as it might well be the last plane out for days. And considering she was in charge of Lauren's rehearsal dinner Friday night, that would be bad. Really, really bad. That frightened her enough to send Julie into a half-run. She shouldn't have agreed to travel this close to the wedding.

She eyed the gate numbers, spotting seven, when she needed eleven. She fought to ignore the pinch of her toes in the black three-inch heels that matched her safe black travel dress, cringing at the sight of huge snowflakes outside the wall of windows to her left. They seemed to fall at an accelerated speed while she watched. Her gaze lifted to the monitors and she cringed yet again at the flashing red with the word 'cancelled' next to a great number of flights.

"Please don't let mine be one of them," she murmured, afraid to stop to check for fear seconds could cost her the seat with her name attached.

Arriving at her gate, the empty waiting room seats emphasised just how late she was for boarding. The doors to the entry ramp were still open, and that meant she'd made it on time.

Eager to confirm she was right, Julie hurried to the counter and presented the attendant behind the counter her ticket. "Please tell me I'm not too late for this flight."

The forty-something woman smiled and pushed the rims of her black glasses back onto her face. "You're in luck. We've boarded the last group, but the flight's been delayed fifteen minutes."

A sigh of relief slid past Julie's lips. "Thank you. And you're right. That's luck because I really need to be on this flight. Do you think I dare sneak away for some food to take on the plane with me before I board?" It was nearly eight at night and divorce negotiations had been so heated, she'd never gotten her sandwich down.

"If you hurry and I do mean hurry," she said. "Rush back."

"I will," Julie promised. "Thank you, again. Please don't let them shut the doors without me."

"I won't," the woman promised. "I'm going to check in with the crew and I'll flag your name as present." The woman rushed away and Julie stuffed her ticket inside her purse, ready to seek out the nearest restaurant.

She made it all of four or five steps before she stumbled over Lord-only-knew-what – a cord of some sort she thought –

and nearly fell flat on her face. She righted her ankle, thankfully avoiding a sprain, but her briefcase took the tumble for her, sliding down her shoulder and hitting the ground. The contents spilled out.

"That's why you should zip it," she mumbled, holding her skirt down to squat in as much of a lady-like fashion as was possible considering the circumstances.

"Need help?"

Julie froze at the sound of a familiar male voice that couldn't possible belong to who she thought it did, when the tingling awareness down her spine told her it was indeed exactly who she thought it was. Luke Walker, the brother of her best friend's soon-to-be husband. Not only did Luke and his two brothers run Walker Security, they held a number of airport consulting contracts, including this one. She squeezed her eyes shut at her predicament, at having the very man she'd avoided at all cost for the last six months standing above her.

Slowly, her gaze lifted, travelling upward in what felt like slow motion. She took in muscular, denim-clad legs, a tapered waist, and an impressive chest. He bent down, a wisp of his dark hair brushing his brow, his rich, chocolate-brown stare capturing hers and leaving her speechless.

Memories of the two of them together, of a too short, heated affair that had happened when he'd been on leave from the SEALs, rushed through her. It had been a safe fling, short-lived, and without the strings and complications that she knew from experience led couples straight to divorce court. But he wasn't a SEAL anymore, and he wasn't leaving this time, and after struggling to shake off the impact he'd had on her ever since they'd parted ways, she'd accepted that nothing about him had ever been safe.

"How are you here when I'm here?" she whispered. The timing was impossible, regardless of his contracts.

"Luck it seems," he said, and those full, sensual lips she knew could be both punishing and soothing in all the right ways, hinted at a smile. "I had a meeting with airport officials that ended just in time to give you a helping hand." He reached for a large file, shoved papers inside, and then rested an elbow on his knee to offer it to her. "Shouldn't you be in New York with the bride-to-be?"

"Yes," she said, stuffing the file in her bag, pretty sure her own Lady Luck was playing games with her tonight. "I should. I got pressured into a negotiation that I regret." She stood up and he followed, handing her one last file that she quickly put into her briefcase. "Thank you for your help."

She couldn't seem to think of what else to say. He was so close she could smell the masculine spice of his cologne. She knew the brand, knew where he sprayed it. And she knew how good it smelled when he was naked and it was the only thing he had on. She shoved the inappropriate and tantalising thought away and reached for something, anything, to say. "Are you on this flight?"

"I guess that's where my luck runs out," he said, glancing at the window before adding, "I'm on the next one out and I'm not optimistic with this weather."

"You have to be back to help with the wedding, too," she insisted. "You're the best man. Can they convince someone to give up a seat for you?"

"The airline tried. There were no takers. I'll get there one way or another, though, even if that means catching a charter flight."

"You can't fly out in some small plane in a dangerous storm," Julie said, alarmed. "Luke, please tell me you won't do that."

"You just said I have to get home."

"You do, but safely."

He arched a brow. "Worried about me?"

"Yes," she said without hesitation. This was one area she wasn't hiding her feelings. "I am worried about you. Very. I know you were a SEAL, but don't be macho. You can crash and die just like the rest of us."

"I'm not macho."

"You Walker men personify macho."

"You must be talking about my brothers," he joked.

"You were a SEAL. That's another way to spell macho."

"I was," he agreed. "But not any more."

Julie discreetly inhaled at the implication of those words, the silent message they held. He was here. He wasn't leaving this time. What was she going to do about it? Those chocolate brown eyes of his held hers, and the air thickened, crackling with sudden awareness. His voice softened, turned velvety. "You know, Julie, we could-"

"Excuse me, Ms. Harrison," the airline attendant interrupted. "You need to board."

"I'm on my way," Julie said, glancing at the woman and then quickly back to Luke, hoping he'd finish his sentence.

He hesitated only an instant, clearly abandoning whatever he'd intended to say. "You better go. See you at the rehearsal dinner. I'll be there. You get on that plane and make sure you're there, too."

"Don't take unnecessary risks," Julie ordered.

"I won't."

"Promise."

"I promise."

She studied him, not sure she believed him. "Luke-"

"Miss," the attendant said, sounding urgent, "your flight is going to leave without you. You really do have to board now."

Julie walked backwards. "Getting killed would ruin the wedding, Luke."

"I know." He chuckled, a deep, sexy sound that tickled every nerve ending she owned. "Get on the plane. I'll see you there. Alive."

She inhaled and forced herself to break eye contact and hurry towards the ramp. She was worried about him, and she told herself that was because of the wedding. It was something to focus on other than what he'd almost said. We could...We could what? It didn't matter. Nothing was going to happen between them. She wouldn't let it.

13

So why with each step did she have to fight the urge to turn and see if Luke was still there. She didn't want to know if he'd tuned her out, when she couldn't forget about him, which was another reason not to turn. Luke was trouble, heartache, misplaced emotions that couldn't end well. She didn't do relationships for a reason. They didn't work. Yet, he made her forget caution, made her want to believe in something, she didn't know what. Lauren and Luke's brother Royce made her want to believe, though. They deserved happily-ever-after. They would be the exception. She believed that, but for most part, love hurt. No one knew that better than she did.

***

Luke Walker watched the only woman who'd ever rocked his world sashaying her sexy little behind toward the plane, remembering another goodbye, and wondering if she was remembering it too. It had been two years ago and he'd been headed back to active duty after a month off and in her arms. She'd taken him to the airport, even walked with him inside. They'd stopped at security and stared at one another, long seconds of silence heavy between them, and he'd been unsure what to say. Their time together had been a short-term thing. They'd both been clear about that, no strings, no tomorrows, but he didn't want it to end. He squeezed his eyes shut, reliving the past.

Julie leaned into him, her hands on his chest, scorching his skin through his shirt. She pressed to her toes and brushed her lips over his and it was all he could do not to kiss her like it was his last kiss in this lifetime. "Don't die, soldier," she whispered. "The world needs more men like you, not less."

He'd wrapped his arms around her and held her close. "And you? What do you need?"

She blinked up at him and he saw the uncertainty in her face for an instant. "One last kiss," she said, her mouth finding his again for a feather light kiss that was over too soon. She pushed out of his arms and turned away, half-running toward the exit. Regret and disappointment filled him.

Luke scrubbed the tension at back of his neck. As time had ticked on, one thing about that day had replayed over and over in his mind. There had been no goodbye.

An announcement sounded over the intercom, snapping Luke back to the present. His flight was cancelled. The doors to Julie's plane hadn't closed. He had a gut feeling she wasn't going anywhere either.

He walked to the counter and found the attendant. "Is this flight going to take off?"

She sighed. "They're trying to get clearance but it's not looking good."

"If they don't, since you put them on the plane, will you put them up in a hotel for the night?"

"We won't pay for the room since weather is an act of God," she said, "but we'll get them to a reserved room if they want it."

"Which hotel?"

"The Royal Blue," she said. "If you're thinking about staying there, I'm not sure that will be possible. The airline reserved a large block of rooms. You should check around quickly before everyone is sold out."

"Understood," Luke said. "Thank you." He turned away and started walking. The airline wasn't the only one with a Royal Blue contract. Airport administration and security had one as well, and he had a security clearance badge that gave him priority reservations. He was headed to the Royal Blue and he wasn't giving Julie a chance to run away to a different hotel.

He'd see her when she arrived.

Chapter Two

An hour and a half after she'd left Luke behind in the airport, Julie was off the plane and inside a hotel, rolling her bag toward the registration desk. She wondered about Luke and where his flight and the night had taken him. She worried about both of them getting home for the wedding. The temptation to call him would have been extreme if she actually had his number, especially since she just might be needing that charter flight to get out of here quickly. But she didn't have his number and she wasn't going to call Lauren and Royce and freak them out about being snowed in when she might well be on an early morning flight. If not, well, she'd find her own charter if she had to, and ignore her own warning issued to Luke to be careful. She'd walk home before she'd miss Lauren's rehearsal dinner.

Julie stopped at the roped-off area to wait in line for registration, noting that there were a good ten people in front of her, most of whom were from her flight. Thankfully, she'd caught the first shuttle to the hotel or the line would probably be longer already.

With a sigh, she leaned on her suitcase, feeling the ache of the long day, and as time ticked by without any movement, she let her lashes lower. Her mind went back to the last time she'd said goodbye to Luke. To that day in the airport when she'd dropped him off. The end of their affair had come far too soon. She told him the world needed more men like him. "What do you need?" he'd asked in response. It had been all she could do not to say, "You, Luke. I need you."

A sudden shiver of foreboding swept down Julie's spine with such intensity that she straightened and cast a furtive glance around the lobby. Her attention was drawn instantly to three men standing with their backs to her near the door to what looked like a restaurant or a bar. They weren't even looking her way and yet...there was something about them.

Elizabeth Moore's words played in her head. "He won't kill me. He won't kill you. But there are others who'll kill us all if they find out what he's hiding." Julie rubbed her arms, inwardly shaking herself for letting her imagination get the best of her.

The line progressed, and she gladly refocused on getting to a room and out of this lobby. Several more customer service reps took their places behind the counter and in a matter of a few minutes, she was being called forward. Still, she found herself casting a glance towards the three men, only to find them gone. So why didn't she feel relieved? In fact, she felt more uneasy.

She didn't have time to contemplate. The customer service rep was quick and Julie was on her way to her room in a snap. She propped her purse on her bag and with key in hand, rolled her way to the elevator, thankfully finding an empty car. She punched her floor and leaned against the mirror, ready for peace and quiet and sleep. Oh yes. Blessed sleep.

A second before the doors would have shut, someone stuck their hand inside the panels and they jerked open with a loud jangle of a bell. That same foreboding chill she'd felt in the lobby travelled her spine.

A man entered the car, his dark stare meeting hers and turning her chill to ice. They were cold, calculating eyes. She cut her gaze and willed her heart to stop trying to jump out of her chest, telling herself to look at him, to get a better description than a tall man, with dark, wavy hair, and a tan jacket, because for some reason she felt she needed it.

He punched a button three floors above hers and she tried to find comfort in that fact. With a destination, a room, and a right to be here, he was likely just another traveller. Still, even with that logic, she counted floors, willing the car to move faster. The doors opened, but not at her stop, and Julie fought the urge to dart forward and just get out of the car.

A young couple rushed forward and joined them. Julie reached for the handle of her bag. She should get off. Get away from the strange man who now held the door for her. But what if he got off, too? There was safety in numbers and she had company now.

The doors started to shut and she let them. One more level up and the couple got out, leaving Julie alone with the stranger, and as uneasy as ever. She stared at the doors, ticking off the seconds until they stopped two levels up. The instant she was able, she rushed forward, eager for escape.

Once Julie was in the hallway, she found her destination a few rooms to her left. *Thank you.* She was nearly to sanctuary and safety.

Letting her bag settle upright on the ground, she glanced over her shoulder, eyeing the elevator. The doors were just now closing with the stranger still inside, she assumed. Still, had the man held the door open long enough to see which room was hers?

Gnawing her bottom lip, she worried despite assuring herself the rooms were safe, and near impossible to break into. Key in hand, she swiped the plastic through the electronic panel, and frowned when the little light stayed red. "Damn," she mumbled as she slid it again.

Still red.

No. No. No. Please say this wasn't happening. She dropped her head to the surface of the door, her hair falling forward, glad it covered her face. Crying wasn't her style, but tears prickled in her eyes. Seeing Luke had rattled her. Add in her fear of missing the wedding and she was a mess. Then there was Elizabeth Moore's visit, which clearly had shaken her to the core. Good gosh, she was tired. She was worried. She was not herself. A return trip to the lobby felt overwhelming.

"Problem?"

The deep, sensual baritone danced along her skin and sparked a familiar, warm feeling. Lifting her head, Julie swivelled around and blinked, thinking her eyes were playing tricks on her.

"Luke?" He was leaning against the door frame of the room next to hers, his light blue t-shirt hugging rippling muscles she'd had the joy of exploring. And it had been a joy. Her mouth went dry, her fatigue doing nothing to dull the impact of his presence. Heat pooled low in her stomach, and her pulse kicked up a beat. The man was even more sexy than she remembered. For the second time in one night, she found herself questioning the crazy coincidence. "How are you here, right next door to me?"

He gave her a half-smile, his left dimple showing, and his chocolaty eyes just a little sharper. "My luck continues despite a flight cancellation." He inclined his chin to indicate her bag. "Need help?"

She exhaled a breath that had somehow lodged in her throat. Luke was dangerous, yes. Dangerous to her heart, to her decision-making. But he made her feel safe on a night when she felt far from it. She didn't know why, just that it was better now that he was here. "My key isn't working. It's been a bad night, but I'm sure you guessed that."

He gave her a thoughtful look as he pushed off the door frame. "Sitting on a runway is no fun. I do believe I got the better end of the deal. I was sitting here, waiting on you to arrive. I reserved your room in advance." He stopped in front of her. Close again. So close.

"You reserved my room, next to yours?"

His eyes darkened, the air crackled. "That's right," he said, closing his hand around her key, his fingers brushing hers and sending heat up her arm. "I thought we might need to plan a way home together and I didn't want to risk upsetting Royce or Lauren by letting them know we were stranded."

"That's what I thought, too," she said. "I thought about calling you for that charter flight but I didn't have your number."

"The dangerous one you warned me not to take?" he asked stepping to her door to swipe her card.

"Yes," she laughed, surprised she had the energy. "The dangerous one. I hear there's a brave Navy SEAL who'll be on it to keep me safe." Oh God, she was flirting. She needed to stop that. Sex was a resource, a tool to keep things recreational for men. Nothing personal. Only it hadn't worked that way with Luke. It hadn't worked that way since Luke. She watched him swipe the key three times. "I tried the door, you know?" She didn't care that he tried again. She'd just been trying to divert attention from her careless comment.

He shrugged. "It never hurts to try again, though in this case it did no good. The key is a dud. At least it's not a grenade. Well, unless the grenade lands at your feet."

"That happened to you?" she asked, delving into the very personal territory she'd sworn not to with this man over and over, but did it anyway.

"Oh yeah," he said. "Fun times, let me tell you. And I checked on a charter. It all depends on how bad the storm is tomorrow. If the weather allows it and the airlines are backed up, it's an option." He grabbed the handle of her bag. "Why don't you call downstairs from my room, and have someone bring you up another key?" He didn't wait for her reply, rolling her bag, with her purse still on top, toward his room.

Julie stood frozen, her eyes fixed on his powerful shoulders and back. If she followed him she was not coming out of that room without touching him.

Desire flared and pressed her to act, countered only by the worries that fluttered through her mind. His brother was marrying her best friend. There was no fling to this. They were headed to a place she'd never let herself go with a man. A place she'd sworn never to go. This was relationship territory.

He stopped at his door, and eyed her over one of those truly magnificent shoulders, a challenge in his watchful gaze. "You gonna stay in the hall, or what?"

She wanted him. Part of her even felt as if she needed him. She shouldn't do this, but.... She shut her eyes a moment. Who was she kidding? Walking away from Luke wasn't possible. That meant she had to find a way to deal with him. Maybe she simply hadn't had time for the sex in their past to get old. Maybe they were only drawn to each other because he'd left before they worked each other out of their systems, and she'd turned this thing with him into more than it had to be. Right. She could take control again. She'd get this back where it belonged. In the bedroom and out of her head and heart. Heart. Damn. Where did that come from? Head. She'd meant head.

Her lashes lifted and she met his gaze. "Or what?" And she followed him into his hotel room.

Chapter Three

Luke was aware of Julie on every possible level, in every inch of his body, all too conscious of just how much willpower this night was going to require. He wanted her. He wanted her like he'd never wanted another woman, and that was exactly why he couldn't touch her. Not now. Not yet. But soon, and he knew it was going to feel like forever in the meantime.

The door slammed behind him and he settled her bag in a corner by the closet, easing into the doorway to watch her sit on his king-sized bed, her long blond hair caressing her shoulders. Shoulders he knew were creamy white, skin he knew was soft and silky, and addictive. She reached for the phone. He leaned on the wall, his blood boiling just thinking about how easily they could end up under the sheets, or on top of them, or anywhere in this room, gloriously naked. The mattress separated them, yet he could smell the faint scent of jasmine and vanilla, a perfume so uniquely Julie.

Oh yeah, he was staying on this side of the mattress, and on the opposite side of the room from Julie. He'd given this thing between the two of them one heck of a lot of consideration and was certain that sex was her barrier, the only thing she gave of herself, the wall that hid her from truly connecting. Only he'd gotten past that wall, he'd seen it in her eyes in the past. He saw it there now: the fear, and the knowledge that he was the man who'd seen the real her.

"Yes," she said into the phone and even her voice radiated along his nerve endings and threatened to unravel his control. "My key won't work. Can someone bring a new one up to me by chance? I'm in my neighbor's room. Room-" She glanced at the phone. "813." She paused and listened, and then sounding disappointed, asked, "That long? Really? Okay. Hmm. Yes. Fine. I'll be down." She hung up the phone and stood up, turning to face him. "They're too busy to come up anytime soon so I have to go down."

"They said that about room service when I tried to order," he commented. "I should have assumed the same for this."

"I guess that means I have to go downstairs now." She ran her hands down her hips and looked nervous rather than her normal sexy confident self. Nervous was good. Nervous meant she was feeling something unfamiliar. It meant she was aware of what was on the line, and it had nothing to do with pleasure. Well, maybe a little to do with pleasure.

Neither of them moved or spoke, the air thick, the bed the size of a Texas summer sun, threatening to burn them right into high noon. He needed out of this tiny room with her and now.

"I don't know about you, but I'm starving," he said, pushing off the wall. "Why don't we head down and get something to eat while the front desk calms down a bit."

She studied him a long moment, as if his invitation to leave the room surprised her far more than the one to join him here.

"I seem to remember you having a big appetite," he pressed softly, reminding her of their time together, of just how well they'd gotten to know each other. Of late night pizzas and walks to the corner deli, and a diner near her house that they'd had many a breakfast at. She wasn't hiding from any of that. She wasn't hiding from him.

Her lashes lowered, and her hair fell forward, shadowing her face. "Yes," she said, drawing out the response before casting him a surprisingly shy look. "I probably like to eat a little too much."

"Says who?" he asked. "Not me. I prefer a woman who actually eats." He motioned to the door. "Shall we?"

She smiled and admitted. "I am hungry."

And so was he. For her.

***

Julie stepped into the elevator with Luke, aware of how big he was, how good he smelled, unsure of what had just happened in that hotel room. She'd thought it would be sex and sin, and forgetting everything but sex and sin. It hadn't happened. She hadn't even tried to make it happen even though she wanted it. His cologne tickled her nostrils, alluring and familiar, intimate simply because she knew it so well. Lord help her, she still loved everything about the man. Discreetly, she took a deep breath and inhaled that scent, unable to stop herself. Neither of them spoke, but it wasn't awkward. Nothing with Luke was awkward aside from how much she wanted him. How differently she wanted him from anyone before him.

When the ding of the elevator signaled they were at ground level, he held the doors and let her step out of the car, reminding her he had always been a perfect gentleman. Something she'd always loved about him. Standing just outside the car she waited for him to follow her.

Luke stepped to Julie's side just as a busty redhead approached. "Hold the elevator, cowboy."

Cowboy? Julie thought with a frown. Luke wasn't a cowboy at all. The woman sashayed past Julie as if she didn't exist, focusing solely on Luke. Her short skirt left little to the imagination, as did her actions. She offered Luke a flirtatious smile and a wink.

He held the elevator door for her and she paused in front of him. "Need someone to keep you warm, honey? I know just how to handle a wicked winter night."

Julie sucked in a soft breath, feeling the bite of the woman's words, unable to stop her reaction. It wasn't like she didn't know how women responded to Luke. He was the proverbial tall, dark, and handsome with a rock-hard body and gorgeous eyes. To make matters worse, the woman was actually quite attractive with legs that could reach to China and a slender, lean body, so very unlike Julie's. Suddenly, Julie felt short and stubby, and lost.

Then, to her utter and complete shock, Luke's arm folded over her shoulder. "This one here is in charge of my wicked winter nights, but thanks anyway."

Feeling his body against hers, the sensitivity of his actions, rather than the implication, warmth rushed over her. He let the door go, but not before she saw disappointment flash on the woman's face. Luke glanced down at her. He dropped his arm and they started to walk. "You could have put your arm around me, too, you know?" he asked, cutting her a sideways look. "I don't bite, and," he grinned, "a guy needs to stay warm."

Without giving herself time to think about her actions, she wrapped her arm through his and gave him her own mischievous smile. "Sometimes you bite."

He laughed. "Maybe I do."

They walked together like that, like a couple, and she remembered doing just this in the past, strolling down a Manhattan sidewalk, chatting on their way to dinner. She remembered how good it had felt, how she'd felt like a part of a couple for the first time in her life. How for a few weeks she let it feel good, too, knowing he'd be gone, knowing there was no risk. Only there had been an aftermath, a change in her she still didn't understand.

The restaurant consisted of empty tables that formed a half circle around a bar. "I guess it's a good thing everyone is at the front desk," Luke said. "We have plenty of seating choices."

"Your choice," confirmed the hostess, who looked maybe eighteen at most, but was probably twenty-one considering the bar, confirmed.

Luke motioned toward the first booth and glanced at Julie. "Work for you?"

"As long as it's close to the kitchen."

The hostess laughed. "Best seat in the place."

"Then it's a winner," Julie confirmed and made her way to the seat facing the exit.

Luke slid in across from her and grabbed a menu, about the same time as a young male waiter appeared. "Drinks?"

Luke quirked a brow at Julie. "Tequila Sunrise?"

He remembered her drink and it pleased her way too much. "Yes," she said without looking at the waiter. "Still a 'Shiner Beer' guy?"

"You bet I am," he said, leaning back and stretching his arms over the seat. "Shiner for me."

"Check," the waiter said, shoving a pencil behind his ear. "Tequila Sunrise for the lady and Shiner for the dude, coming up." He headed out, one of the many pins with funny sayings clipped to the front of his yellow and black striped apron falling to the ground in his wake. Julie bent down and scooped it up.

She checked the weather on her cell phone. "It says the snow is supposed to stop around two in the morning. I sure hope they're right."

"Me too," he said. "We are both cutting it short."

"Why are you here so close to the wedding?" she asked.

"I had ticked off a client that I didn't want Royce to find out about before the wedding. I'm guessing you had a divorce emergency?"

"Divorce of the rich and famous," she said. "It's not a pretty business, but it's what I do."

"You might not have planned to be a divorce attorney," he said, already knowing her story, "but it sure seems to be treating you right. I hear you've become a regular Hollywood star."

"Not Hollywood," she said. "Mostly athletes. I handled one player and they all flocked to me. Same stories I'm used to, but more money and nastiness in the breakups. That's just how divorce goes down."

"More demands from the clients on you too, I assume?"

"Oh yes. In this case, not only was the wife threatening a tell-all book my client didn't want to see light, the threat was all over the tabloids. I didn't want to risk this escalating any more than it had to, smack in the middle of the wedding." Of course, now she faced another problem with Judge Moore that might hit her in the face at the wrong time.

The waiter set their drinks in front of them. "Ready to order?"

Julie hadn't even opened her menu but she knew what she wanted. "How about a cheeseburger well-done and fries?"

"Ditto for me," Luke agreed and exchanged a few casual words with the waiter before they were alone again, and his attention returned to her. "So, back to your reason for being here. I'm guessing from the tabloids you're here for New York's star pitcher David Rodriguez's divorce?"

She gave a nod. "Yes. His ex is from Chicago."

"So is he," Luke said, and then spat off some random David Rodriguez stats and Julie arched a brow that had him adding, "Did I mention I'm a David Rodriguez fan? Big, big fan."

"I'm not." The man hit on everything with a skirt including her. "And if you knew the man personally, you wouldn't be either. And if you repeat that, I'll deny it. There were plenty of reasons that man didn't want a tell-all book to be published. Things he, fortunately, had enough sense to not want his ten year old daughter to ever find out, or have to deal with, publicly."

Luke tipped back his beer and studied her a long moment. "You came here because you were worried about the daughter, not because David demanded you come."

His ability to read her so easily flustered her. He saw too much, and she told herself to ignore his comment, but for reasons she didn't understand, she found herself saying, "Yes. Because I was worried about the daughter."

"Because you know what divorce does to a kid."

She sipped her drink. "I have a little experience in that area, yes. Parents involved in divorce are often so wrapped up in their own pain they forget their actions have long term effects on the kids." A swell of discomfort formed in her chest. She didn't want to talk about this. "You're lucky. Your parents stayed together."

"Forty years," he said. "My mother is dating again." He shook his head. "I can hardly get my head around it."

"But it's also been three years since your father passed," she said and their eyes met, and she knew he was remembering two years before, and the night he'd told her about his father, his hero, dying of a heart attack. They'd been at a Japanese restaurant drinking sake and laughing when things had turned serious. It had been the night that she'd known she was in unfamiliar waters with this man, that she felt so much more for him than just attraction.

"Yes," he finally agreed. "Three years ago last month." His lips curved. "I guess that means she's allowed to date. And he's a nice guy. A retired school teacher who lives down the road from her in Jersey. A real scholarly type who is night and day from my career military father."

"Maybe she needed night and day to move on," Julie suggested thoughtfully.

"Maybe," he conceded. "I suppose that's true." He took a drink of his beer. "Blake doesn't like the guy."

"You said he was nice."

He laughed. "That's why Blake doesn't like him. He says no one is that nice."

"Cynical, isn't he?"

"Aren't you?"

She didn't even try to deny the truth. "Yes. I am."

He arched a brow. "That was an easy confession."

"I'm a divorce attorney."

"And maid of honor at your best friend's wedding. That can't be an easy match."

"My job is incentive for the groom to be sure he keeps the bride happy. And he'd better or I'll personally kick his ass. Screw divorce court."

He chuckled. "I don't think you have to worry about that. Lauren turns my big grumpy brother into a teddy bear. But if Royce screws this up, I'll help you kick his ass. She's good for him. He needs her."

"In contradiction to my cynicism, I believe she needs him, too."

The waiter showed up with the food and they both dug in. "I'm curious," Julie said, after a small silence to enjoy a bite of her surprisingly good burger. "Why did you leave the SEALs? You were so adamant about being career Navy."

He poured ketchup on his plate and then motioned to hers, and she nodded, letting him put some on her plate too. "The official story," he said, "is that I had an injury to my leg."

"The unofficial story?"

"It healed, but Blake is a loose cannon, damaged and in a big way."

"His fiancée was killed on an ATF mission," she said. "I heard."

"And he's a time bomb waiting on his chance to explode. He wants vengeance to the point of absolute obsession. It's why he left the ATF. He wants it at all costs; he'll even ignore the law."

"And you intend to do what?"

"Keep him alive."

"Royce couldn't have done that?"

"My brothers would die for each other, but most of the time, they also want to kill each other."

She inhaled and let it out. "I see. That's...intense. And honorable, Luke. I know how much the SEALs meant to you. You—" That same shiver of foreboding slid down her spine and her gaze lifted to find the man from the elevator at the hostess stand. His eyes met hers and then suddenly he stalked toward their table. Julie did something she never did under pressure. She froze.

Chapter Four

Y ou dropped your phone, miss," the man said in a heavy Spanish accent, squatting down beside her and offering her phone, his hand on Julie's chair for balance.

Julie let out a breath that she didn't even know she'd been holding, because for the past two seconds, she'd pretty much didn't know anything but panic. Her phone. Right. Which she probably knocked off the table when she'd picked up the waiter's pin. Or while distracted by Luke, which was pretty much always.

Thank you," she said, accepting her cell from the stranger, but not looking at him. Her spine was buzzing with ridiculous unease. The man was just helping her. "I had no idea I dropped it."

"My pleasure to help," he said, and pushed to his feet and left.

Julie held the phone, staring down at it. What was wrong with her? This wasn't like her at all.

"What just happened," Luke prodded urgently. "What upset you?"

She shook her head. "Nothing." She refocused on Luke, glad he was here. "I'm just tired."

"No," he insisted. "That man upset you."

"No, I-"

"Yes," he said. "And if you don't tell me why, I'll go find out myself. I've never seen you like this." He started to get up.

"No. Wait. Luke. Please stay here. I'm just embarrassed. It's me being paranoid."

He relaxed back into his seat. "You don't need to ever be embarrassed with me, Julie. And you aren't a paranoid person. If something feels wrong to you, it probably is."

"Maybe," she agreed. "But not here or with that man. I think one of my cases has me worried and it's got me seeing demons everywhere."

"Talk to me, sweetheart."

She inhaled and let it out. "I can't." But she wanted to. She really wanted someone's advice and Lauren didn't need this right now. "Client-attorney privilege."

He scooted his plate aside. "Do you have a dollar?"

Her brows furrowed and she reached for her purse. "Well, yes. Sure. I always carry cash when I travel." She pulled out a bill and slid it on the table.

"Great," he said. "Walker Security is now your private investigation firm. We are bound by privacy laws as well. So talk to me."

Relief washed over her. "I actually think that hiring you might be exactly what I need to do." She told him the entire story about Elizabeth's visit.

"Blake was ATF," he said when she'd finished. "They deal with art theft and money laundering so I'll want to get him involved in this."

"Money laundering?" she asked, the idea opening up all kinds of new concerns for her. "That's what you think is going on?"

"What do you think is going on? You're close to this. You must have had some initial thought pop into your head when Elizabeth made this claim."

"My fear was some sort of illicit pornography."

"That's certainly a possibility, but one thing is for sure. You don't want to be accused of covering it up. Ignorance has benefits when it comes to the law in this case."

"But I'm not ignorant when I've been warned," she said, "so I need to know what it going on."

"You could drop out of the case."

"I could," she said, "but I could still be connected, or even become a fall guy. I've seen some nasty things since I started practicing. I'd rather be on the offensive and be sure this goes away for me."

"That makes sense," he said, "and while Elizabeth thinks her husband isn't capable of hurting her, or you for that matter, I've seen some things myself. Desperation brings out the worst in people."

"I saw that in Elizabeth. It worried me."

"What worries me more than anything," he said. "is this other party who'd be dangerous if they found out whatever the secret is. If this is something illicit, and the wrong person—"

"I'm in trouble."

"I didn't say that."

"You were going to."

"No," he corrected. "I was going to say you could be linked to something really nasty that you don't want to be. There's no reason to get as worked up as you are, though, when you know nothing right now about what is really going on. But it doesn't hurt to be cautious either. I'm going to get Blake on this tonight and look into it more myself when we get home."

She swiped hair behind her ear. "Thank you, Luke. I'm really glad things worked out like they did and I ended up telling you about this. I didn't want to bring it up to Lauren and Royce right now. Not with the wedding coming up." And Lauren was her family, the only real person she counted on. The one person she would say anything to, admit anything to.

"I'm a friend, Julie," he said. "I hope you'll remember that. You can come to me. I'll help you."

Friend. That word changed everything between them. You didn't have a fling with a friend. You had a relationship. She smiled through the tight ball of emotion coiling in her gut at that claim. "Be careful what you wish for," she teased. "I might take you up on that and ask you to, oh I don't know, do some manly thing like put brakes on my car."

"You don't have a car."

"I might get one."

"You don't want to pay $600 a month to park it, any more than you can stand to sit in traffic rather than take the subway."

"You don't forget anything do you?"

"Nothing," he said softly. "Especially where you're concerned."

The confession took her off guard and left her tongue-tied. Where had the sexy seductress persona she'd created to deal with men gone to? And why did his confession make that ball of emotion in her chest turn into a boulder? "Maybe you should," she said, knowing they were on dangerous territory, desperate to find safe ground, justifying that desperation with the fact that Lauren was marrying his brother.

"I tried to forget," he said. "It didn't work."

He'd tried and it didn't work? What did that mean? She didn't get the chance to ask. He tossed cash on the table, including the dollar she'd given him. "How about we get out of here?"

She shook herself inside and told herself it didn't matter what he meant. She pushed to her feet. "Yeah. Let's get out of here." This didn't have to be about emotions. They were in each other's heads. The best way to fix that was to stop talking. Talking complicated things. Talking led to emotion, to heartache, to places she didn't want to go. It was way past time to get back to the hotel room. They'd work each other out of their systems and move on. Maybe then, when this burn they created in each other was through, they really could be friends.

***

The crowd at the front desk had thinned and it didn't take Julie long to get what she needed. In a matter of minutes, she and Luke were at her room. She swiped the new key and received a green light.

"It works," she said, smiling. "Excellent."

33

"I'll grab your things," Luke said, disappearing and reappearing quickly. She held her door open as he rolled her bag inside. Once she'd joined him and let the door shut behind them, nerves tightened her throat and sent flutters through her stomach, belying the idea that sex with Luke somehow gave her control. She didn't feel in control at all.

He settled the suitcase in the corner by the desk and turned to face her. "We'll want to be at the airport early to be sure we're on the first flight out. I say we should leave no later than eight."

"Should we go earlier?"

"I called and talked to a contact at the airport," he said. "Nothing is leaving before ten."

"Okay then, yes. That sounds good."

He motioned to a separate door that connected their rooms. "Knock if you need me."

He intended to leave, she realized with surprise. This wasn't how she thought this night would end. Maybe he wanted her to show she wanted him. Maybe he thought they were a complication he didn't want, regardless of the connection. She'd certainly thought that as well. That should come with relief, but it didn't. Not at all. "I'll be fine. Thanks for everything."

"Just the same," he said. "You know I'm close." He grabbed his cell from his belt. "We should also exchange numbers."

"Right. Yes." Julie dropped her purse to the bed and pulled her phone from inside. "I'm ready."

Once they'd traded cell phone numbers, he stepped closer, less than an arm's reach away. She could smell him, could all but taste him. "I should let you rest," he said.

"Okay," she said, not sure what else to say.

"Make sure you lock your door."

She nodded. "Right. Yes." She mentally cringed at the words she'd said just minutes before. Apparently, her witty attorney mind had already gone to bed for the night.

He stared down at her with dark, unreadable eyes. His gaze drifted to her lips, then lifted. He was thinking about kissing her. She wanted him to kiss her. Heat radiated off of him, calling to her. She told herself to act, to move. Why wasn't she moving? Getting this back where it belonged.

"Good night, Julie," he finally said, brushing his fingers down her cheek, sending a whole different kind of shiver down her spine. And then, just like that, he was gone, already at the door, and ordering, "Come lock up," a moment before she heard it slam behind him.

Julie did as he said, fighting the urge to call his name and drag him onto the bed. It was too late. He was gone. She flipped the lock and let her back settle against the door.

This was good. No complications. It's what she wanted, the way she lived. It was what was right. Only, it didn't feel right at all.

**

Luke had stood in Julie's room, hot, hard, and all about stripping her down and hearing her moan his name, but he'd somehow walked away. He'd left her behind. He'd succeeded in sticking to his plan to see where this thing between them would lead, besides the bedroom. He'd also ensured sleep was impossible.

By dawn, he was out of bed. Thirty minutes later he was showered, dressed in jeans and a t-shirt, and packed to leave. He spent the next hour and a half researching Judge Moore, and his connections, and passing along leads by email to Blake.

By seven, determined to keep Julie from running off without him, fairly confident that's what she would do, he was at her door with two cups of steaming coffee in hand. He'd seen the confusion on her face, and he knew she wasn't sure how to deal with him outside the bedroom. She'd figure it out. He'd help her. They'd figure it out together. He'd show her they weren't the sum of their passion, but rather their passion was a sum of much more that she wasn't ready to put a name to. He wasn't sure he was either, but they had to do something because avoiding each other wasn't an option. Their lives were too intermingled.

He knocked on her door with his foot, the idea of seeing her again shooting fire through his veins. He stood there a minute and kicked at the door again. No answer. He cursed, knowing he'd been right about her leaving him behind, and she'd still outsmarted him. She was gone, probably while he'd been sitting at his computer.

Luke set the coffee by her door so he didn't spill it all over himself and headed back to his room. He dialed the front desk and sure enough, she'd checked out. Well, she wasn't going anywhere without him. He'd already pulled strings and made sure they were on the same flight going home, seated next to each other.

***

Forty-five minutes later, Luke was inside the airport, past security, and searching for Julie. He spotted her at counter of one of the gates, the dark blue jeans she wore accenting her curves, her long blond hair loose around her slender shoulders, and the short-sleeved red silk blouse showing off her pearly white skin. She was gorgeous. She also seemed to be flustered, as was the customer service rep, and since he was pretty sure he was the cause, he hurried toward them.

"I don't understand how you put all those other people on a flight out but you say my name isn't on that ledger. I recognize most of them from my flight." Julie was asking the lady as Luke appeared beside her, and settled his hand on Julie's back. Her head swung around in surprise. "Luke?"

He grinned at her. "Not expecting me, I guess?" She looked guilty. Luke looked at the service rep, whom he'd met several times. "Sue, how are you?"

The twenty-something woman smiled and flipped her dark hair over her shoulders. "Hey Luke, I'm good," she said with a flirty little grin.

"I'm glad to hear it," he said with a smile. "I believe you should have a reservation for myself and Ms. Harrison on the next flight, under a special security clearance."

"What?" Julie asked, turning to him. "What reservation?"

"I would have told you if I had the chance," he said. "I pulled some strings to get us on the first flight out."

"No," Julie insisted. "They just called those names and I wasn't one of them."

"Actually," Sue said. "You are on the first flight out. It's a reserved flight for priority travelers. I missed the reservation because of the way it was flagged by Luke's name."

Luke arched a brow at Julie. "Now would be the time to have your seat moved away from mine if you want to."

Her expression softened. "I don't want that."

"You sure about that?"

Pink flooded her cheeks. "Yes. I'm sure."

"Here you go," Sue said. "Two tickets. You're all set."

Luke held Julie's stare a moment and then accepted the tickets. "Thanks, Sue."

"We should begin boarding in about fifteen minutes," she informed them.

"Excellent," he said, and he and Julie stepped away from the counter, where he teasingly asked, "How about some coffee? I'm guessing you haven't had your standard two cups of coffee this morning, since you took off from your room so early."

"Luke, I-"

"Don't know what to do about me," he finished for her. "Ditto me about you, but I'm betting we don't have a chance of figuring it out without some caffeine."

She sighed. "I'll buy. It's the least I can do considering you got us on this flight and I, well, you know."

"I know," he said, not about to let her off the hook for running off and leaving him at the hotel. "And since I brought you coffee when I showed up at your door this morning, I'll let you provide this round."

"You brought me coffee?"

"That's right."

She glanced at a clock. "You showed up early."

"You left earlier."

"You knew what I was going to do."

"Just not how early." He lowered his voice. "I know you better than you think."

Surprise flashed on her face before she quickly joked, "Then you know I'm dangerous without coffee." She started walking.

Luke smiled and followed. She was still running, but he had a good feeling he was catching up.

A few minutes later, they sat down in the waiting area, cups in hand. She sipped her white mocha. "I still don't know how you drink your coffee straight-up black."

"It's the only way I got it the past few years," he said.

"I remember you saying that," she commented, settling fully into her seat and crossing her legs. "You're a civilian now though. We need to convert you to a real coffee drinker."

"What can I say?" He leaned back to bring his gaze level with hers. "I know what I like." And he liked her.

Awareness thickened between them. "I remember that about you, too," she said softly.

"What else do you remember?"

She traced her lips with her tongue, pulling his gaze down to their glistening wetness. Hunger rose inside him, the need to kiss her, to taste her. To know her as he once had.

Her lashes fluttered, long and dark against her pale cheeks, before she surprised him by confessing, "I remember a lot of things."

"Good," he said. "Then we can compare memories."

Her eyes opened and she met his gaze. The warmth and desire he saw there punched him in the gut. The sexual tension between them was going to kill him. He ached for her, burned for her.

Her cell phone rang. Neither of them moved. It rang again. She swallowed hard. "I should get that. My assistant and I were playing phone tag this morning."

He grabbed her purse and handed it to her. She retrieved her phone. "It's her." She hit the answer button and he watched shock roll over her face. "Dead?" She sat straight up. "How? When?""

"Who?" Luke asked, having a bad feeling he knew the answer.

Julie cast him a worried look and she covered the phone. "Elizabeth Moore. They say she committed suicide and....I just can't believe it. Luke, she's...dead."

Luke inhaled a sharp breath. Just what had Julie been dragged into?

"Consciously or not, greed and power are deadly partners."

Chapter Five

L uke texted Blake while Julie finished her call to her assistant, telling him of Elizabeth Moore's death. Blake's reply was typical Blake. "Holy shit, man, you know how to find trouble. How'd you stay alive in the jungles without me?"

Normally, he'd have replied with some brotherly love like ATF does research while SEALs get their man, but now wasn't one of those moments. Instead, he said, "Worried about Julie's involvement." And Blake had replied, "Enough said. I'm on it now. And no, before you say it, I won't tell the bride and groom."

Julie ended her call and immediately hit a button before he could stop her. "I have to reach the judge," she said. "The funeral is tomorrow. That's fast. Can a funeral even happen that fast?"

"Apparently they can," he said, assuming they were cremating the body, too. "Let me guess. She overdosed?"

"Yes. How'd you know?"

"Still on that lucky streak."

"Voice mail," she said, and quickly left an urgent message before saying, "Luke, she wasn't suicidal. If anything she was fighting to survive." The boarding announcement for their flight sounded and Julie grimaced. "I really wanted to talk to the judge before the flight."

"Maybe you shouldn't," Luke said. "You're upset and you need to handle him cautiously. You need to distance yourself from this for all kinds of reasons, namely your safety."

"I should have done more," she fretted. "I should have—"

"Don't do that to yourself," he insisted, his hand settling on her leg. "You didn't have anything to go on but her threat."

She turned to him. "Yes, but—"

He leaned in and kissed her, determined to give her something else to think about. Her lips were soft, delicate, perfect and what was meant to be a brush of his mouth to hers became a lingering caress. "No buts," he whispered, brushing her hair from her face. "You aren't to blame for her death."

Her teeth scraped her lip. "I can't turn a blind eye to this, Luke. It's not who I am."

"I'll find out what happened. You have my word." He leaned back to study her. "Trust me to do that. I won't let you down."

The boarding call sounded again, but still they didn't move. He held his breath, waiting for her reply, knowing trust wasn't something Julie gave easily, and not to anyone he knew of but Lauren.

"Yes," she finally said. "Okay. Thank you, Luke."

"Good," he said, and while this wasn't how he wanted to take a step forward with Julie, it was still a step. He drew her hand in his and they stood up. "Let's go home."

She nodded. "Yes. Home sounds good and safe."

Luke just hoped she was right about that. He wasn't so sure.

***

Julie could still taste Luke's kiss on her lips as she settled into a window seat and adjusted her seat belt. He slid in beside her, his knee brushing hers, making her heart flutter in her chest. She was confused about Luke and tormented about Elizabeth. She replayed the meeting in her office, tried to think of what else she should have, or could have, done. She should have done something.

"Julie," he said, trying to get her attention, and she realized she was staring blindly out of the window.

Her head whipped around. "I have to go to the funeral."

He drew her hand in his. "Honey, relax."

"I'm trying and failing," she said, and she didn't have it in her to pull her hand away, to fight this thing with Luke, to protect herself from heartache. "This is so not normal for me."

He reached up and brushed his knuckles gently across her cheek. "I know that. You know the wedding rehearsal and dinner is tomorrow night."

"Yes, but I took off of work tomorrow so I should have time for both."

"I'll go with you to the funeral."

She shifted in her seat to face him. "You don't have to do that."

"I want to come with you."

She wanted him to. Oh God, she so wanted him to. Warning bells went off in her head. This was headed to heartache. She was vulnerable right now, raw and open, and— "I'll be fine by myself."

"I'm going with you."

"No. I need to go by myself." She didn't want to start depending on Luke and lose her ability to stand on her own.

"You need me there with you," he said softly. "And if you aren't willing to admit that, I'm fine with that. But I need to be there with you. I'm in this with you and I'm staying in."

"You don't have to do this, Luke. You have no obligation—"

"Who said anything about obligation?"

"I'm Lauren's best friend, and—"

He kissed her again, his fingers curling around her neck, his tongue flickering into her mouth for one brief taste. "I'm not going to let you deal with this alone."

She didn't know how to reply. Alone was all she knew. Alone was where she'd end up after they were over and she didn't want to forget how to be that way and still be happy. Her stomach suddenly churned and she knew it was stress and lack of sleep.

She sank down in her chair. "I'm not feeling so good all of the sudden." She glanced at him.

"Do you want me to get you a Sprite?"

"No. Thank you." She let her lashes lower. "I need to rest my eyes."

Luke ran his hand over her hand. "Rest, sweetheart," he said. "Sleep will do you good."

Yes. Sleep. When was the last time she'd slept well? Not since before Elizabeth Moore visited her office. She inhaled, drawing in Luke's comforting scent, and drifted off.

***

Julie felt a tickle against her ear, but she tried to ignore it. She was wrapped in a warm cocoon of sleep and comfort.

"Julie, wake up."

"Hmm, I don't want to," she replied and snuggled further against... Her eyes popped open. Her senses were instantly alert, her nose filling with the spicy male scent of Luke. She blinked and slowly looked up, her lids still heavy from sleep.

Luke stared down at her with his gorgeous, chocolate brown eyes.

Suddenly she realized she lay in the crook of his arm, her hand on his chest, and her head on his shoulder. Her memory slowly returned as she glanced around and realized she was on a plane. She wasn't sure how she had ended up sleeping in his arms but her subconscious mind seemed to know exactly where she wanted to be.

Slowly, he lowered his head and brushed his lips across hers. Once, twice, and then a third time in short, soft caresses.

Her lashes fluttered to her cheeks as she absorbed the pressure of his lips with warm acceptance. Oh god, she had missed him. He made her feel so much, so deeply, and no matter how it scared her, she needed this, needed him.

"Luke?" she whispered, not sure it wasn't a dream.

His lips quirked. "Expecting someone else? We're about to land. I didn't want the jolt to scare you."

"Um," she said forcing herself to move away from him and sit up. "Thanks."

"How do you feel?" he asked.

"Better," she said, the funny feeling in her stomach now gone. "A lot better. I've never handled sleep deprivation well. It just about killed me in law school. I guess I should thank you for being my pillow."

"Then I guess I owe you the same thank you," he said. "I fell asleep, too."

They'd slept curled up together like a couple and clearly she'd slept like a baby. She turned to the window, the runway fast approaching. They were almost home all right, and most definitely out of one-night-stand-land, she knew that now. She wasn't pretending otherwise. But she needed some time to process it, to figure out what it meant, and how to respond. She'd never let herself consider going where she seemed to be headed with Luke. She either had to dare to let it happen or she had to shut it down. Both had consequences she had to consider, especially with Lauren being her only close friend, her only family. Luke was about to be her family as well.

Once they were off the plane, Julie tried to make her escape, but Luke didn't let it happen. He was with her at baggage claim and with her in the cab line.

When a car pulled forward, she turned to say goodbye to Luke, only to find him giving both her bag and his to the driver. "You live across town from me," she said.

"I'm coming by your place to check things out," he said. "Just to be safe."

"I'm going to my office."

"After you stop by your house, right?"

"Yes," she admitted reluctantly.

"Then let me check it out just to be safe."

She considered arguing, but it was a problem she hadn't considered. Her house being dangerous. Someone there, waiting on her, to make her dead like they had Elizabeth. She slid into the car without complaint.

"You're making me paranoid," she whispered when they were on the road.

"You said you were already feeling paranoid."

"You're making it worse."

"Come stay the night with me."

She laughed. "Right. Like that would raise some eyebrows. You live in a private building with your two brothers and Lauren."

"They all know we have something between us."

"I'm not staying with you tonight."

"Fine then," he said. "I'll sleep on your couch."

"You're not sleeping on my couch."

"We can talk about it later."

"There's nothing to talk about," she insisted.

"You're right. There isn't."

"Luke—"

He kissed her, stealing her words with a hot caress of his tongue. "Stop doing that," she ordered, pressing her hands against his chest and wishing he'd do it again.

"Is that what you really want?"

"It's what's smart."

"Says who?" he challenged.

"Probably the cab driver."

"There's a glass and we're G-rated compared to what he sees on an average night in Manhattan. I want to know what you want."

"This isn't like the last time," she said.

"No," he agreed. "I'm here to stay."

"And you're about to be Lauren's brother-in-law."

45

"Which means what?"

"We're complicated."

"What in life isn't?"

Her brows dipped. "You have an answer for everything, don't you?"

"Except how to get you to admit you want me to kiss you again."

"I didn't say I didn't want to. I said it wasn't smart."

He kissed her again. "Seems pretty smart to me." He pulled her close. "Feels pretty smart to me, too."

Her hand settled on his chest, his name a whisper on her lips. "Luke."

He smiled and kissed her again. "I know. The cab driver." He released her and gently stroked hair from her eyes. "Seems like we have a lot to talk about later."

She sank back into her seat and didn't reply. She had never been so confused in her life. One minute she thought hopping back into the bed was the right answer. The next, she thought it was the completely wrong answer. The truth was, she didn't know what to do about Luke, but she had to do something.

***

A few minutes later, they were at her apartment door. Julie pushed it open, and they stepped inside. Luke tugged both of their bags in the door and leaned them against the wall. Cici, her white oriental shorthair cat, was instantly up the three steps to the foyer at Luke's feet, purring and rubbing all over him. "I think she missed me," he said, bending down to pet the cat.

"Apparently, she didn't miss me," Julie said, squatting down beside him to stroke Cici. "Little wench has always had the hots for you."

"At least I've won over one woman in the house."

He'd won her over, too, but she wasn't going to say that. "Because you play with that bird toy she loves with her." She pushed to her feet and he followed. "Am I safe to move around the cabin, Captain? Cici is going to want to be fed."

"Give me a chance to have a quick look around," he said before he headed down the stairs.

Julie leaned against the door, wondering how she'd gone from avoiding him to having him in her house. She wondered why she couldn't just make this about sex and enjoy the hot man currently searching her bedroom. What made Luke different? He sauntered toward her with a sexy, loose-legged swagger, and a confidence about him that brought the one-word answer to her question to her mind. Everything. The answer was everything about this man made him different.

Before she knew his intent, he was in front of her, his hands sliding into her hair. "You were wrong in the cab when you said this time is different."

Those words punched her in the chest. This was more to her than him. "I was?"

"Yeah, you were," he said. "We were just as good then as we are now." He brushed his lips over hers. "See you tonight." He grabbed his bag and was out the door before she could think what to say or do. The door shut, and she sank against the wall. Cici appeared again and began rubbing her leg.

Julie sank down to the ground and ran her hand over Cici's head. "What are we going to do about him, kitty?"

Cici purred and meowed, and Julie imagined her saying 'Can we keep him?' "You're no help," Julie said with a grimace. "You're kitty putty in his hands." Julie sighed. And she wasn't much better herself.

She grabbed her purse to punch in Lauren's number.

"You're home! I was worried sick," Lauren exclaimed.

"I'm home, so don't worry," she said. "I'm taking care of everything for tomorrow night." She hesitated. "I was thinking though it would be fun to have a girl's night two nights in a row, instead of just the night before the wedding. I could stay with you tonight or you with me and we could do up the gift bags together."

"I was thinking the same thing," Lauren said. "It's silly because we never fight, but I have this fear Royce and I will fight and decide to call off the wedding. Or maybe we'll have really bad sex and that will make the wedding night really awkward."

Julie laughed. "Fighting and really bad sex don't fit the Lauren and Royce I know, but it's a date. My place or yours?"

"Yours," she said. "But, can you swing by after work and help me get everything to a cab and over there?"

"Of course," Julie said. "I'll see you there say, about four? I'm taking off work early."

"Perfect."

Julie ended the call and inhaled deeply. She was being a big chicken, but she didn't care. She really did want to spend time with Lauren. In fact, she wanted to very badly. The problem was, she could easily say the same thing about Luke.

***

Later that afternoon, Luke still had Julie on his mind, more than a little eager to see her again. He sauntered down the hallway of the apartment building he and his brothers had bought and renovated several years ago to both work and live in, carrying a tuxedo for Royce. He stopped at the door at the far end of the hall, two doors down from his, and knocked. Used to be he'd just walk into Royce's place, but since Lauren had moved in, he was sensitive to their privacy.

The door opened and to his surprise there stood the woman of his recent, and not so recent, dreams. His lips curved in a knowing smile. "Decided to stay the night?"

"Actually," she said. "Lauren's staying with me."

"Not when Royce finds out what's going on," he said. "He, like me, will be concerned about safety."

She stepped into the hall and shut the door, her blue eyes lit with urgency. "Luke, she wants to stay at my place to build up the anticipation before the wedding. I don't want to tell her no.

48

Please don't involve Royce in this mess I'm in and get both of them all worked up about this. Lauren will worry herself sick about me and now is not a time for her to worry."

"You stay here at their place," he said. "Tell her you want her to be comfortable. Royce can stay with me. He'll stay away if that keeps Lauren happy."

"But—"

"Now is also not a time for anyone to get hurt as you pointed out at the airport," he said. "Be safe, not sorry."

She sighed and nodded. "Okay. You're right. To be honest, I've been thinking about it ever since she and I decided this and I thought about calling you."

He arched a brow. "And?"

"I was still thinking about it when you showed up at the door."

"Is that right?"

"Yes. I would have called." She crossed her arms in front of her. "Probably."

"Not," he supplied. "Did you talk to the judge?"

She shook her head. "He won't return my calls. Did you find out anything?"

"Nothing worth telling yet." He lifted the tuxedo. "I'll take this back to my place. Is Royce here?"

She shook her head. "He's at the limo service fixing some mix up."

"I'll call him and work things out," he said, and smiled, lowering his voice. "There's an easier way to deal with me than avoiding me."

"What? I wasn't..." her voice trailed off, and she shoved a lock of that silky blonde hair behind her delicate earlobe. "And that would be what?"

He gave her a wicked smile. "Don't." He turned and headed back down the hallway, feeling her watching him, and wishing he could just drag her to his place and make love to her. But as his SEAL commander used to drill into their heads, 'patience is a virtue' and Luke had learned to make it work for him. Every instinct he'd honed over the years said this was one of those times when slow was better than fast.

Chapter Six

Once Luke knew Julie was safely at Lauren's place, he headed to the offices of Walker Security on the ground floor of their building to meet with Blake. Royce was taking a shower and then the three of them planned to head out for beer and pizza at their favorite joint up the road.

"Anything?" Luke asked, shoving open the door and finding Blake behind one of the four desks facing each other in pairs.

Blake leaned back, his hands behind his head where his long hair was tied at the nape. "The judge has his records sealed fairly tightly," he said. "But not tight enough for me not to get past them. I just need more time that we don't have right now." Luke perched on the edge of the desk across from Blake as his brother continued, "As it stands, since our guy Jesse was NYPD for years, I put him on the judge," Blake continued, "Kyle is the tech guy so he's following up on the electronic trails. We don't have the manpower to dig into her family right now. We're too stretched, but I'll do it when the wedding is behind us. I already tapped his phones at home and work. One thing that stands out so far is that he's got an offshore account – that is never a good sign."

"He could have been hiding money from his wife," Luke said, thinking his brother might be messed up in the head, but he was damn good at his job. "They were, after all, getting divorced."

"She was broke and struggling," Blake confirmed, "so no doubt, but I'm guessing we'll find out it's more than that."

Luke ran his hand over the knot of tension at the back of his neck. "Yeah, me too. Otherwise the wife wouldn't be dead.

And I can tell you right now that Julie isn't going to let this go. She feels responsible for Elizabeth Moore's death."

"Speaking of Elizabeth Moore," Blake said, sitting up and tapping a pen on the desk. "She was cremated, as you said, and the public is only being allowed at a short cemetery service. This happened way too quickly. The body was examined and prepared in a window that is nearly impossible. Someone pulled strings to make that happen."

"Someone powerful like the judge," Luke supplied. "That was exactly my thought, too."

"Just to be safe, you need to keep Julie close," Blake warned. "I don't know what it is us about us Walker men, but the women in our lives tend to end up in trouble or dead."

"I plan to," he said, thinking there might be some truth to his words. Luke knew he was talking about more than his dead fiancee. Lauren had been in some trouble months back that had almost gotten her killed. "Can you keep Royce busy during the funeral? The last thing I need is getting him all worked up over this."

"I hear ya on that one," Blake said. "I'll work something out with him over dinner."

Luke looked up the details on the funeral and dialed Julie, knowing she wouldn't back down about attending. She answered on the first ring.

"Hello." She sounded surprised. "Something wrong?"

A lot, but he didn't say that. "Just calling to confirm the time for the funeral. It's at two tomorrow. We're only allowed to attend the outdoor ceremony."

"That's odd," she said. "Or is it? I don't really know what is normal for a funeral."

"It's odd," he confirmed. "Another reason I'm coming with you."

"Won't Royce be suspicious if we disappeared together dressed in black?"

"I'm handling Royce if you have Lauren taken care of."

"She's going to the spa," she said and hesitated. "You don't have to–"

"I'm going," he said, "so don't sneak away without me. I'll show up anyway."

He could almost hear her frown. "You're being very pushy."

"I am," he agreed, giving Blake his back and lowering his voice. "But this is about your safety so I'm not going to apologize."

She hesitated. "All right. I'll see you at 1:30."

Luke ended the call with a goodbye just as Royce stalked into the room, bigger and burlier than his brothers, with his hair long and tied at the nape like Blake's. "I'd rather drink beer and eat pizza at home. Actually, I'd rather be at home with Lauren."

Blake pushed to his feet. "Yeah yeah, you grumpy ass, we know. But you can't throw Lauren over your shoulder and run to your cave until after the wedding. We're going to have fun whether you like it or not."

And Luke was going to keep Julie safe, whether she liked it or not. It was the one thing in their relationship he considered non-negotiable.

***

It was 1:25 p.m. the next day and Julie had managed to send Lauren on her way to the spa without her, giving an excuse about taking care of last minute dinner details. At the sound of the bell, Julie rushed to open the door, feeling her knees go weak at the sight of Luke. His silky black hair fell over his forehead and dipped down to his strong brow. The man did for a dark suit and long coat what an engagement ring did for a bride's finger. He made it look like perfection that couldn't be undone.

"I'm ready," she said, slipping her purse over her shoulder. "Or as ready as I will ever be for a funeral. Everything is set for the rehearsal dinner. We'll just have to change before we show up, so we don't look like we've been to a funeral. Some people think black is bad luck for weddings."

"You don't?"

"When it comes to marriage, I say don't trust luck or fate to be in our favor. We should change."

"I'm all about getting more comfortable," he said, "but right now, you're going to need a coat." He gave her simple black dress a once over that was so hot that she might argue his point, until he added, "It might not be snowing like in Chicago, but the wind is vicious and cold today."

And they were only invited to the outdoor cemetery service which she found odd, but then, she didn't know much about normal when it came to funerals.

"Right, thanks. I'm a wreck trying to organize tonight on top of this." She reached behind the door to the coat rack and grabbed her long wool jacket. He reached forward to help her put it on and they ended up with his hands on her lapels. She stared into brown eyes that had her melting like chocolate.

"You don't have to do this today," he said softly.

"I do," she insisted. "I have to."

He considered her a moment. "Have you talked to the judge?"

She shook her head. "He never returned my call, but I figure that part is probably expected."

"I wish you'd reconsider this," he said. "I don't want you any closer to this situation than you have to be when we don't know what's really going on."

"You keep rephrasing that and saying it over and over."

"And I'll probably say it at least one more time before we get to the cemetery."

"It feels important to me."

He brushed the hair from her brow, his expression and his voice turning gentle. "Then it's important to me."

Her throat went dry and her breath caught in her throat. Men had told her she was beautiful, told her she was sexy. Told her they wanted to pleasure her. Things all women knew that men said when they wanted to get a woman into bed and keep her there. No man had ever made something as grim as a funeral, or for that matter anything she cared about, important just because it was important to her.

He seemed to sense her loss of words and stepped back to give her room. "Let's get this over and move on to the wedding bliss, shall we?"

"Yes, please," she said, pulling the door shut behind her and then locking it. "Where is Royce?"

"Blake took him to the shooting range for me, so he wouldn't ask questions, and because he was climbing the walls with pre-wedding jitters."

They started the walk to the stairs and she wondered what it would be like to have siblings that came through for you like Luke did. "I owe Blake a few thank yous it seems."

He snorted. "Blake likes holding a gun almost as much as he does a different woman every night."

"I've gathered from being around him that he's a real player."

"Fast women, fast cars, and danger," he said. "He's an adrenaline junkie since Sara died, trying to feel something aside from pain."

She cast him a sideways look as he held open a door to the private parking area to their building, which was a rare find in Manhattan. "You're really worried about him, aren't you?"

"Blake is like jogging with a bomb in your hand," he said. "He's going to explode, it's just a matter of when and how badly, which is exactly what he thinks about the Elizabeth Moore situation." He clicked the lock on his Black Dodge Ram. "Let me help you up. The step is high." He opened the door.

"Does that mean that you've uncovered something concerning?"

"Elizabeth Moore ending up dead after she threatened her husband is plenty in my book," he said, "and we have a couple of our best men digging around. We'll know more after the wedding."

Julie sensed he wasn't telling her everything. "If Blake is a bomb certain to explode on a scale of 1-10, where does he rank?"

"Seven on a good day. Nine on the other 364."

"And this situation?"

His expression remained unchanged, emotionless, but the several seconds of hesitation was almost as telling as his answer. "Eleven."

***

They pulled up to the cemetery only twenty minutes later, and that was because of bad traffic, the wind gusting, and the sky gray and threatening. Julie had never been to a cemetery before. She hadn't even been to a funeral. She had no real family, so it was one dark spot in life she'd really never faced. Dread clawed in her stomach at the sight of the tombstones.

Luke pulled the truck to a stop behind a line of parked cars and Julie could see the tent across the terrain. Guilt twisted in her gut. Why hadn't she called the police? Because you had nothing to offer them, she reminded herself.

"You aren't responsible," he said, accurately reading her thoughts. "There was no way you could have foreseen such a thing."

"I appreciate you saying that more than you know," she said, running her suddenly clammy hands down the fabric of her dress.

"We can—"

"I'm staying," she finished before he could.

He sighed. "I'll come around and help you out."

She waited on him gladly, feeling out of sorts. Uneasy and wobbly. Luke being here helped, and while on a personal level that might scare her, it also made her stronger.

Luke opened the door, and she turned to let him help her down, and blurted, before she could lose her nerve. "Thank you. I'm glad you came."

He stared at her for a long, moment, his face unreadable, before he gave her one of those sexy smiles that made even the dread in her stomach fade for a moment. With the ease of lifting a grocery bag, he lifted her and set her on her feet, running his hand down her hair. He did that a lot and she liked it way too much.

"Let's go get this over with so we can happily marry off Royce and Lauren."

"Yes," she said. "Please. I want to go back to Lauren's fairytale land. It's nicer there."

He slid his hand down her arm and surprised her by twining his fingers with hers. Silently, they fell into step and for the second time in her life, she had a sense of being part of something good, something right, something that was at odds with what she believed was in her future and even the grim, bitter cold of a day at the cemetery.

Droplets began to fall and Luke quickly pulled them into the back of the surprisingly large tent, a good fifty-plus people in seats. Sobs filled the air, and the rain picked up, the wind splattering it against the tent fabric. The judge sat in the front row, but she didn't recognize those close to him. What got to Julie the most was the absence of a casket. There was a much smaller finely etched wooden box that she assumed held what was left of the beautiful, too young to die, Elizabeth Moore.

It wasn't long before a man in a robe stepped forward to a podium and began to speak. The wind seemed to howl at the same moment, as if Elizabeth herself was protesting her demise. The darkness of the event, the sadness surrounding her, tightened Julie's throat, and she felt the prickle of tears.

Luke pulled her under his arm, and she happily took the shelter he offered. The next fifteen minutes was a blur that felt endless.

When the final prayer ended, the crowd scattered. People went to the flowers in a center display for Elizabeth, while Julie clung to Luke's arm, just staring at them.

"You okay?" he whispered in her ear.

She swallowed and nodded, turning to him, tears burning in the back of her eyes. "I'm fine. I've never gone to a funeral before."

He covered her hand where it had landed on his chest. "It's not a good experience. Ready to go?"

"More than ready." They started to turn and Julie paused. "Should I say something to Judge Moore?"

Luke stared down at her, his eyes heavy with concern. "If you want to, we will."

We. She liked that 'we' right now. She shouldn't. It was dangerous but she just couldn't get herself to care. Her gaze lifted to where the judge still sat in his seat, unmoving like stone. Giving her condolences seemed appropriate, but she suddenly realized she wasn't here for Judge Moore. She was here for his dead wife and she wasn't sure she wouldn't go off the deep end and confront him. That would be bad. Very bad.

Decision made, Julie shook her head. "I want to go."

Approval lit his eyes and he took her hand to lead her out of the tent. Julie collided with someone. She pulled back, started by the impact, only to find herself sucking in a breath at the sight of Elizabeth Moore.

Chapter Seven

The woman who was Elizabeth Moore, but wasn't Elizabeth Moore, slid her hand into Julie's. "Thank you for coming to pay your respects to my sister," she said, and then she was gone. Stunned, Julie realized the woman had pressed a piece of paper in her hand.

Discreetly, Julie turned to face Luke. She reached down and put her hand in her coat pocket. "Let's go now, please."

"It's raining hard," he warned.

Her gaze swept the terrain outside the tent and indeed, it was pouring rain. "I don't care."

He gave her a keen look and took her hand. "I'm in for cold and wet if you are."

They darted into the rain and he helped her into the truck. When he finally climbed in, her teeth were chattering.

"My heater is a furnace," he said, cranking the engine. "It'll be warm in a minute." He glanced at her. "I didn't know Elizabeth had a twin."

Julie shoved her wet hair from her face. "Me either. It was a shock. They're identical."

Suddenly, he pulled her close and kissed her and all that ice and dread inside her thawed. She needed that warmth, his warmth, more than she needed to breathe right now. And while she was melting from the wicked heat of his tongue, he reached into her pocket and pulled out the note.

He leaned back and held it up.

Feeling defensive, she quirked, "I would have told you if you'd have given me the chance."

His lips thinned in obvious doubt as he read the note. "We have to talk." He glanced up at her. "That's it and a phone number." He shoved it in his pocket. "I'll take care of this. After the wedding."

"You're being obnoxiously domineering," she said. "I don't like it."

"And I like you better alive," he said. "So if you want to be mad at me, I'll take the anger."

"What if someone else is in danger, Luke? What if—"

He kissed her again, and damn it, she managed to resist a whole two seconds before she all but moaned from the feel of his mouth on hers. The man was making her crazy, taking control of her life. "Don't do this to yourself," he ordered softly. "I'll have someone find out more about her sister right away. I promise. You just focus on the wedding."

"You promise?" she confirmed. "Because if anyone else ends up dead, I'll never live with myself."

"I promise, and I never break a promise."

She swallowed against the sudden dryness in her throat, because not only did she trust him, she realized she trusted Luke as she never had any other man. "We should go."

Julie scooted out of his arms to face forward, confusion filling her. He acted like a big brother with kissing privileges, and avoided every chance he'd had to get her naked and in bed. She didn't understand. Did he want her or not? And why did it matter to the point that it hurt thinking that he might not? What else explained his quick hotel departure, or leaving her apartment where they'd been alone with barely a kiss? Or suggesting he sleep on her couch not in her bed with her?

***

Several hours later Julie had donned a pale blue dress the color of the wedding theme. She'd headed to the church, where she'd spent the entire rehearsal avoiding eye contact with Luke, feeling every touch of Luke's hand as they practiced walking down the aisle. She didn't know what she was feeling or how to deal with it. She just didn't know.

Avoiding eye contact at the dinner afterward proved more difficult. The group of twenty sat in a private back room of Eden, a favorite Walker restaurant. It lived up to its name with vines, flowers, and spectacular plants covering the ceilings and the walls.

Julie sat on one side of the long triangular table, to the left of the bride, while the groom was to her right. Luke had chosen a seat directly across from Julie, and beside him was Blake. Every time Julie looked at Luke she was struck by how delectable he looked in a royal blue button-down. Which was why, among other reasons, she kept her attention on Lauren. But she could feel Luke watching her, feel the tingle of awareness that touched every place his gaze landed.

Julie leaned in close to Lauren and discreetly indicated to her recently divorced father, a retired senator, chatting away with her soon to be husband's mom. "Someone should warn him she's seeing someone."

"Oh good grief," Lauren said. "Royce and my father are only just now starting to get along." She slid out of her seat and headed over to her father, squatting down beside him.

Luke's sexy rumble of laughter caught her attention and Julie's eyes darted on their own accord toward him. A young brunette waitress with deep cleavage was blatantly flirting with him, and he seemed to be enjoying the attention.

Instantly, Julie felt the unfamiliar and very unwelcome flare of jealousy, the same feeling she'd felt in the hotel.

"Julie?"

Her eyes darted to Lauren, and she didn't even realize Lauren had returned. "Sweetie," Lauren said, "what's going on with you and Luke? I know you don't like me to bring up your past with him, but it is obvious something's going on with you two."

"We're friends," she said quickly, not wanting to talk about herself. Tonight was about Lauren. "Nothing more, and all is well."

Lauren took a sip of her wine and studied Julie closely. "Maybe later tonight, when we're alone, you might want to talk."

Julie forced a smile. "About you and your soon-to-be hot new husband. You're marrying the man you love tomorrow. I know you went to the spa today, but you never get your feet done, so I bought pedicure stuff, lotion, and candles."

Lauren smiled brightly and gave Julie a big hug. "I love you, you know?"

Julie smiled into her hair, fighting emotion. "I love you, too."

Feeling ever weepy, Julie let a busboy take her salad plate and reached for her wine, only to realize that her hand was shaking. She set the drink back down and somehow her gaze collided with Luke's right when the waitress settled her hand on his shoulder.

Breaking eye contact, she diverted her gaze to the plate that had just been set in front of her. Suddenly the crowd was suffocating her. She needed space. Tossing down her napkin, she scooted her chair away from the table and excused herself. Making a beeline to the bathroom, her steps were hurried, her heart racing ridiculously fast for no explainable reason.

Thankful for a bathroom that held only one, Julie yanked the door open to step inside. The last thing she needed was an audience of women. Suddenly, she felt hands on her waist as she was lifted forward and sat back down in the bathroom. The door slammed, and she whirled around to see Luke locking the door.

***

Luke turned to find Julie gaping at him. "Are you crazy, Luke?" she demanded.

"Depends who you ask and on what day of the week, but not now, no. Now, I'm real darn clear on what I'm doing and why. I've known that waitress for years. She's a friend, and nothing more."

She hugged herself, turning away from him. "I have no clue what you're talking about, Luke."

He took a step forward, slid a finger under her chin and forced her gaze to his. "You were upset when you left the table."

"No, I...it's been a confusing scary few days. I'm not myself."

Her hand went to his wrist and heat darted up his arm, but it was the vulnerable, insecure look on her face that undid him. She didn't think he wanted her. Despite his attention, despite the kisses that would, and should have, set off a five-alarm blaze, she didn't know.

He slid his hand to her neck. "I only want one woman and that's you."

"Then act like it, Luke," she said, "because you're confusing me and I don't know what you want. I–"

He covered her mouth with his and for the first time since his return, he let her taste his desire, let her feel the hunger inside him that no one had sated since her. His hand slid over the sexy curve of her hip to the dip of her tiny waist.

Her arms wrapped around his neck, and she molded herself to his body. She was no longer vulnerable or timid. She was the seductress she could be, the seductress he knew had just lured him to the very place he'd sworn he wouldn't go. To the land of lust and forgetfulness where she ruled, where sex was a weapon, and a wall of separation grew despite the absence of clothing.

She covered his hand with hers, and led it to her breast, molding it to her body. His cock thickened, his zipper stretched. He'd wanted this woman for ages, and the days of turning away from her, from wanting her and not having her, had left him on edge and hungry.

He tore his mouth from hers, his chest rising and falling, his breathing heavy. Her eyes were dark, heavy-lidded, her gorgeous perfect mouth swollen from his kisses. "I swore I wouldn't let you do this to me."

"What is it I'm doing?" she asked, her hand sliding down his zipper to stroke his erection. "This?"

"Yes," he said, giving her the same treatment she had him, pressing her hand down on his crotch. "This. What am I doing to you, I wonder?" He shoved her skirt up, his finger trailing over thigh highs that told him her stellar ass would be all but naked. "Are you wet, Julie?"

She leaned in, her lips a breath from his. "Only one way to find out."

His cock thickened, his zipper strained even further. He slanted his mouth over hers, devouring her, tasting her, when he really wanted to gobble her up. His hands slid around her backside, pulling her close to him, molding her against him, her soft curves against his burning hot and hard body. He lifted her and set her on the counter, her skirt hiked to her waist. Luke pulled back to study her glazed, sexy stare, watching her as his palms caressed a path up her thighs, until his thumbs brushed the tiny piece of silk some might call panties. He called them a tease.

She worried her bottom lip and he felt that scrape of her teeth in every inch of his body. He soothed it with his tongue, his fingers pressing beneath the silk to find the slick heat of her arousal. "Hot and wet," he murmured next to her ear, the scent of her perfume mixed with aroused female working a number on his already revved up hormones.

A knock sounded on the door, and Luke ignored it, kissing her, sliding a finger inside her. Whoever it was would go away.

"Julie, sweetie, are you in there?"

Luke froze at the sound of Lauren's voice permeating the wooden divide between them and her. Julie stiffened and pressed her hands to his shoulders. They drew apart slightly, their eyes colliding, hers filled with panic. Luke reluctantly slid his hand from her body.

A knock came again. "Julie?"

Luke lifted her and set her on the ground, watching her fret over pulling her skirt down. "Yes, I'm here."

His gaze slid over her, and he had to say he was thankful her dress seemed to be wrinkle-resistant or they'd have a much harder time leaving this bathroom.

A long moment of silence. "You okay?"

"Yes," she said quickly. "I'm fine. I'll be right out."

Silence.

Julie's brows dipped. Luke started to say something, but she stopped him, placing two fingers to his lips and holding up a finger from her other hand.

Then came Lauren's voice again. "Um, Julie?"

"Yeah?" she said, meeting Luke's curious gaze.

"Luke wouldn't happen to be in there with you, would he? Royce is, um, well, worried about him."

That was when the full implication of what he'd done, how he'd lost control, hit him like a concrete block. Luke squeezed his eyes shut, angry at himself. He was in a public bathroom about to get naked with the very woman he swore he wouldn't touch until she admitted he meant more than sex to her. And he was doing it during his brother's rehearsal dinner.

Julie tugged on his hand and made a silent plea for help. He shook his head, not knowing the best response.

Lauren seemed to make her own assumptions. "Okay then. As long as we know you're both okay."

Luke dropped his head onto his hand. Fuck!

"Oh, God," Julie whispered, "I can't believe I let this happen."

The torment in her voice drew his sharp probe, and he watched her turn to the mirror to fix her face and hair. He stopped behind her, framed her body with his. Their eyes met in the mirror. "It happened," he said. "We can't change that. It's been a rough day and we were both feeling it."

Her gaze dropped to the sink and he read the instant withdrawal in her, the return of the vulnerability that had set him off in the first place. He turned her to face him. "I didn't say I didn't want that to happen, Julie, but now, and like this, no." He kissed her and when he pulled back she ran her fingers over his mouth.

"You have all the lipstick I no longer have on me on you."

"I'm not complaining."

"I am," she said, and pressed her mouth to his. "I need it back."

He smiled and motioned. "Let's go back."

"We're going to be obvious if we go back together."

"I have a plan." He reached for the door and she grabbed his hand. "You still have my lipstick." She reached up and wiped his face. "I doubt that fits your plan."

"No," he said softly. "But you do." And before she had time to react, he opened the door and checked for a quick exit. The coast was clear, and he motioned her forward. She rushed into the hall and all but ran for the exit, as if she didn't want to be found in damning territory.

As they cleared the hallway and made their way back to the table, Luke made an announcement. "Cake crisis averted."

Lauren looked alarmed as Julie sat down next to her, and Luke quickly supplied the answer. "The bakery wasn't going to get the cakes to the reception in time, so Julie was ordering me to pick them up tonight."

"Oh no," Lauren said. "Are you sure it's okay now?"

"Absolutely," Julie assured her, grabbing her hand. "They had us mixed up with a different wedding." She laughed. "That's why Luke and I ran off." She cast him a warning look that had a hint of 'thank you' hidden within. "You weren't supposed to know." She turned a softer expression on Lauren. "It's handled. Everything is handled. You just have to walk down the aisle and marry the man you love."

She made it sound easy, as easy as it would have been for him to take her right there in that bathroom. He thought of the intensity of her vulnerability, of how quickly she'd shifted from that softer Julie to seductress, and he knew what wasn't easy at all: figuring out how to crack the mystery that was Julie's heart. And he was ready to admit that not only did he want to, he intended to.

Chapter Eight

With the rehearsal dinner behind them, Julie and Lauren sat on Lauren's sofa with a box of double-dutch chocolate cookies. Lauren brushed her hands together to wipe away the crumbs and gave Julie an astute, probing stare. "You seem bothered by something."

Julie glanced at Lauren, the friend who'd become her sister, emotion welling inside her. "I'm fine." She forced a smile. "I'm allowed to be nervous over the wedding, but you are not."

Lauren shook her head. "It's not the wedding. You're not yourself."

Julie shrugged. "Divorce is more depressing than usual with a spectacular wedding in the air."

Lauren quirked a brow. "That's a different point of view for you. You've always been very unemotional about what you do."

"Yes, well, Judge Moore's wife committing suicide really got to me."

Lauren was quiet a long moment. "Yes, I imagine it would anyone. They run in our circles. It's heartbreaking."

Julie didn't want to bother Lauren with her concerns over what she thought really happened to the judge's wife, not the night before her wedding. She waved it off. "A conversation for later. Much later."

Lauren didn't look convinced. In fact, she shoved a lock of light brown hair behind her ear and studied Julie more intently. "Leaving the District Attorney's office to go out on my own with a couple of friends was a huge decision for me. I thought I was fighting for what was right and wrong, but I was tied down by the politics of the office. You didn't choose divorce. It just happened to you, and Julie, it's not a good place for you. We both know it messes with your head, even when you pretend it doesn't." Julie started to object and Lauren held up a hand. "Don't deny it, or you'll make me mad on the eve of my wedding. Look, Julie, why not come with us, and choose what you want to do?"

Julie had already been through this in her head a million times. "The money is good where I'm at."

"Money isn't everything."

"I have no one but me to take care of me," Julie argued. "It has to be a consideration."

"You have me, Julie. You will always have me."

"I know," Julie said, emotion clogging her throat. But Lauren would have her husband, kids, a future, and even though Lauren wouldn't say that changed anything, it did. And Julie was happy for her. If anyone deserved a true fairy tale, it was Lauren. Julie smiled. "And I'll borrow your big grumpy wonderful man to change a light bulb here and there, I promise."

Julie's cell phone buzzed with a text and she grabbed it off the table. It was from Luke. Elizabeth moved in with her sister in Jersey after the split. They're close. Blake has one of our men checking her out and watching her. She's safe.

Julie quickly typed, Thank you.

Lauren cocked her head. "Speaking of the restaurant and Royce's family tree. Seems like you have a big Walker man of your own on your hands these days." She pursed her lips. "Was that Luke texting you?"

Julie was so taken off-guard she just stared at Lauren. Lauren laughed. "It was. I knew it. And so we're clear, I played along on the whole cake thing, but I didn't buy it for a minute. You two were in the bathroom doing the—"

"No, we were not!" Julie exclaimed. They'd just come close. "Are you calling Luke a liar, Lauren? That's rough stuff considering he's about to be your brother-in-law."

"Come on," Lauren prodded, her voice softening. "For once, talk to me about Luke instead of shutting down when I try. Consider it a wedding present."

Julie pulled her bare feet to the leather couch and rested her chin on her knees. "I can't talk about what I don't understand."

"He matters to you," Lauren said, and it wasn't a question.

"He's about to be your brother-in-law," she said, avoiding a direct reply. "That's trouble waiting to happen."

"You're both grown adults. You can be around each other if something doesn't work out."

Julie snorted. "Adults who break up rarely act like adults."

"You're making an excuse to avoid him when you don't want to avoid him at all," Lauren said. "And honey, I'll tell you right now that since the first time you were with Luke, you've changed. He's in your head and you can't ignore that. Deal with it one way or the other."

It was true. She'd changed in so many ways. "Since Luke…" Her words trailed off and she zipped her lips. This was not the Julie 'boo-hoo' show tonight. She sat up and grabbed a bag of cookies from the table, then smacked the box against the one Lauren had set on the couch. "Eat and let's talk about your wedding, not me."

Lauren started to object and Julie added, "Don't make me go down the road and get Ben and Jerry's ice cream."

Lauren held up her hands in acceptance. "I'll never fit in my dress if you go that far. I'll eat cookies. Just don't hide in the bathroom with the best man right before the ceremony, okay? At least wait until after."

"Fine," Julie laughed. "After." And she tried to put Luke out of her mind. But couldn't. Later, when she and Lauren had snuggled into their beds, with the wedding only hours away, she lay there thinking of him. Of the kisses, the touches, of how he'd said 'if it's important to you, then it's important to me.'

She had no idea what got into her, but she grabbed her phone and typed a text to Luke. Thank you.

He texted back almost immediately. For what?

Still being the kind of man the world needs more of, she thought, but instead she typed, Everything.

And his reply, Anything for you, Sweetheart, gave her a funny feeling in her chest that she didn't want to try to identify.

***

The wedding was held at Pier Sixty off New York's Hudson River, the spectacular views enjoyed by all the guests. Julie, like four other girls, was dressed in a pale blue sheath, but only she was allowed in Lauren's private room before the ceremony.

"What if I trip going down the aisle?" Lauren asked, wringing her hands. "I mean, my father has politicians from all over the country out there."

Julie's lips turned up in a smile. "I have no doubt Royce will catch you. And this day isn't about your father. It's about you and Royce."

Lauren nodded. "I know. I know. And when I see him I'll forget the rest." She scrutinized her appearance in the mirror, "Are you sure my make-up isn't too dark?"

Julie walked up to Lauren, carefully avoiding her long skirt, and put her arm over her shoulder. Lauren was a princess in a full, sleek figure-hugging skirt that flared mermaid style. "Look at you," Julie whispered. "You're stunning."

Lauren made a weak effort at a smile. "You think?"

"I know," she said, her gaze tracing the auburn ringlets around Lauren's face. "Your hair is so beautiful like this. The diamond-studded headband and sheer veil will be as perfect as the dress." Julie softened her voice. "He loves you like a man needs to love a woman to marry her. It's special, Lauren. You two are special together."

Lauren gave a sad smile. "I wish my mother was alive for today."

Julie took Lauren's hand in hers, thinking of how close Lauren had been to a mother stolen too young by cancer. "She's here," Julie said. "She's here and she approves."

Lauren turned to Julie and tried to hug her and Julie backed up, waving a finger. "Your hair and your makeup. We hug after pictures." A knock sounded on the door.

"Five minute warning."

Ten minutes later, Julie stepped into the foyer outside the wedding venue, and slid her arm inside Luke's in preparation to walk down the aisle. When their eyes connected, she felt it clear to her toes. She felt...something she'd never felt in her life, something unidentifiable.

"You look beautiful," he murmured softly.

Her lips curved. "You clean up pretty nicely yourself there, cowboy," she whispered, giving a teasing reference to the redhead's remark a few nights before.

He chuckled low in his throat. "And tonight is a cold winter's night."

She smiled at the inference that she should keep him warm as the music began to play. A short walk later, Julie's eyes pinched with tears as she watched the faces of the bride and groom fill with love. For the first time in her life, she believed in marriage.

***

The bride did not fall down as she had feared, but the bride's maid of honor did cry. Julie stood inside the elegant reception hall. It was filled with tables decorated in the same shades of blue and white silk that framed the ceiling-to-floor windows overlooking the river. There was a fire burning in a corner stone hearth, and long tables of food lined the walls, the scents of yummy treats lacing the air. The entire scene held a romantic, warm feeling as perfect as the couple who had just been married.

Feeling emotions she found more than a little unsettling, Julie watched as Lauren and Royce had their picture taken for the millionth time since the day started. They were happy, in love, and ready to be alone. A person would have to be blind to miss the scorching eye contact the two kept making.

She walked to a window, a sense of happiness and loneliness filling her that was at odds with the hundreds of people around her. She never spoke to her mother, and hadn't seen her father since she was a small child. Her grandmother was dead. She was alone.

"What are you thinking?" Luke said stepping up beside her as he settled his hand on the small of her back. A shiver of awareness rushed down her spine. He had taken advantage of every chance he could to touch her throughout the events of the day and she couldn't say that she was sorry.

She turned to face him, carefully masking her emotions. "That they really love each other."

Luke looked at his brother and new wife who stood not far away, and then back at Julie. "Yes," he said thoughtfully. "I believe they do."

She looked down, breaking eye contact with him as her mask started to slip. Luke made her feel things she didn't understand. These last few days she'd been one big bubble of out-of-character emotions.

Luke gently tipped her chin up making her look into his eyes. "You okay?"

He was so confident, so sure of who and what he was. She'd thought she was, too, but her world was spinning out of control, and she barely recognized herself right now. A part of her wanted to let go for the first time in her adult life and lean on Luke, but the past few days reminded her how important it was to stand on her own. He made her forget that, and she couldn't afford to forget.

"I'm just...tired," she said, turning away from him again, before she said something she'd regret. She stared out at the water rather than into his soft brown eyes. They made her want to throw caution to the wind and just get lost in him. But Luke did what Luke always did. He refused to be dismissed.

The call for the cake cutting was announced on the microphone.

"Come," Luke said and took her hand. "We can't miss the cake. You like sweets too much for that." He pulled her along with him and even put a huge clump of his icing on her plate. She laughed and gave him a chunk of her cake. That he knew her so well, and she him, made her chest feel funny.

When it came time for the bride and groom to dance, Luke slipped his arm around her waist. "We're next."

A few moments later she was on the dance floor, in his arms, their bodies so close their legs brushed, the heat of his body seeping into hers. "This is where you belong," he murmured near her ear.

"On a dance floor?"

"Anywhere in my arms," he murmured softly.

Her breath hitched in her throat, and fell from her lips on his name. "Luke–"

His lips pressed closer to her ear, his voice low and raspy. "You know I'm not letting you go home alone tonight. It could be dangerous."

He was dangerous, but she didn't say that, because, well, she couldn't speak. The music turned slow and seductive and his hands settled possessively on her lower back, his hips nestled more firmly against hers. Her eyes fluttered shut as she rested her head on his chest. For just a few minutes, she wanted to forget the future, and the past. She wanted to simply enjoy the man who held her.

Laughter beside them drew their attention, breaking the sweet spell she burned to hold on to. Julie lifted her head and shared a moment of regret with Luke before turning toward the noise.

Blake was dancing with a rather tipsy, bosomy, redhead, and Julie wondered what it was about red haired women this past week.

"Hey, Luke," Blake said and inclined his chin at Julie. "Julie. This is Farah."

The woman smiled at Blake. "Sarah," she said, "But for you honey, I'll be Farah or whoever you want me to be."

"That's how I like my women," Blake teased. "Agreeable." He grinned at Julie. "Well, I guess I'll make an exception for you and Lauren, Julie. Neither of you are ever agreeable." Then he winked and twirled the woman in his arms into the crowd.

Julie shook her head laughing softly. "Fast cars and fast women, eh?" she asked.

Luke nodded and smiled faintly. "That's my brother."

"Not you?"

"No," he said, a solemn quality to his voice. "I'm not like Blake. I've had my share of fun, but I was never like him. Like I said, Blake has something very personal he's dealing with that is his story to tell, not mine, but it seems to have impacted about how he feels about relationships. A lot like you, Julie."

Julie stiffened, feeling instantly defensive. "Don't pretend to know what motivates my actions."

He stared down at her, unblinking in his assessment of her features. "You're saying I'm wrong?" he asked with a soft challenge in his tone. "I don't think so." Julie tried to push out of his arms. "Don't go." His expression was intense, his jaw tight. "I just want you to let go, Julie. I just want you to let me in."

The song ended and again, Julie tried to step out of his arms, but he held her firmly. "Running again?"

"I never ran," she whispered, as the new song started to play, and she seemed to have lost control of her tongue because she said, "You left."

"Not by choice," he insisted. "And you sure didn't stop me."

"You had to leave," she argued.

"That's my point," he said. "Yet, you threw it out there like I chose to go."

He had. He'd chosen to leave without asking for more, without fighting to stay in contact. She didn't want to talk about this. She didn't want to care, to remember, to...

They were standing in the middle of the dance floor, the only ones not moving, and she was acutely aware of how close they were to making a scene. "If we are going to stand here, then let's dance."

He pulled her close again, wrapped his arm fully around her waist, their bodies beginning to sway. "I'm not leaving this time. You have to deal with me."

She didn't even know what to say to that. "Deal with you?" she challenged.

"That's right," he said. "I'm here, sweetheart. What are you going to do with me?"

What was she going to do with him? A part of her reveled in that question, the part that had wondered at his desire for her, the part that still didn't understand what he wanted from her or what she wanted from him. The answer had seemed so simple at one point. She'd have an affair with Luke, she'd enjoy him and send him off to the Navy. Now, she didn't know.

"I think I'd prefer to contemplate that with a glass of champagne in my hand."

He stopped moving, his expression unreadable as he stared down at her. Without a word, he drew her hand in his, and led her toward a bar. When he handed her a tall glass filled with bubbling liquid, she said, "You really don't have to stay by my side all night, Luke. I know there are plenty of people who want to see you."

"Trying to get rid of me?" he asked as he focused his eyes on hers. "That's not the way to deal with me, I promise you."

"No," she said as her pulse kicked up a beat. "I'm not trying to get rid of you, Luke." She was shocked at how much she meant the words, how much she didn't want to get rid of him, how much she didn't want him to let her get rid of him.

His eyes softened instantly. Her surrender had been clear, his approval certain. He set his glass down. Then he took hers and set it down as well. "Come with me."

She let him lead her to wherever he intended, shocked when the destination was his mother's side.

"Mom, you know Julie, of course." His hand stayed on her back as if they were a couple.

His mother, Eleanor Walker, smiled. There was sweetness to her features, a softness that spoke of happiness. She was a pretty woman, even in her sixties, her brown eyes so like Luke's they were spellbinding.

"Yes," Eleanor said, smiling. "You look lovely, Julie. I am so glad Lauren has such a good friend, and you did a marvelous job helping with the wedding." Her gaze slid to Royce and Lauren and she sighed. "Royce can be such a hard man, but when he looks at Lauren I see softness and love." Her gaze moved to the happy couple for a moment, and then flickered across to Luke and Julie. "What's your story, dear? Are you from here? And where are your parents?"

Her stomach clenched and Luke's hand moved to her waist, gently tightening there. "My family's not as close as yours."

Luke's mother stared at her a long moment, a thoughtful expression on her face. "Then I'm glad you have us, dear."

Julie was completely blown away by the statement. She didn't have them. Did she? She had Lauren. Before she could completely digest the words and respond, Senator Reynolds, Lauren's father, appeared.

"Eleanor, my dear, let's dance." The Senator, who knew Julie well, gave her a quick wink.

Eleanor smiled. "You never get tired, but I do, so only one more dance."

The senator looked at Julie and Luke. "Have fun you two."

Julie smiled as they moved to the dance floor, both grinning like children. She looked up at Luke. "They are cute together."

Luke made a face. "She's already seeing someone."

Julie laughed. "I'm sure she's just enjoying the party."

"I want her to be happy, but another man in her life, to be completely honest, doesn't thrill me."

Julie giggled. "She's just dancing with him."

Luke didn't laugh. He didn't smile. He stared at her, his eyes suddenly so intense, she gulped. He took her hand and started walking, pulling her along with him.

She didn't question him. Never got the chance. He was full speed ahead. Before she knew it, she was in a dark hallway. Luke leaned against the wall, feet spread wide as he pulled Julie into an embrace. He slid one hand around her waist, and the other behind her neck as her hands rested on his chest.

Their lips touched in a gentle brush, a feather-light caress so tender she felt a shiver clear to her toes. "Luke," she whispered.

"Um," he murmured as brushed his lips across hers again. "You taste like chocolate icing."

"And you taste like chocolate cake."

He smiled against her lips, brushing gentle knuckles down her cheek. "You aren't alone, you know. My mom was right. You have us. You have me."

He didn't give her time to respond. He took her mouth fully under his, dipping his tongue into her mouth with slow thoroughness, tasting her, tempting her, making her melt. His hands pressed her closer, making her ache with heat as the hardness of his frame seemed to consume her softness.

When he lifted his mouth from hers, his voice was husky as he said, "I swore I wouldn't touch you. Not yet. Not now, but I am coming home with you tonight."

Not now and not yet? She wanted to question his choice of words, but she didn't. Not now. Not yet. Maybe not ever. Instead, she reveled in familiar territory, a place she had some of the control with Luke she desperately needed. "To sleep on my couch?"

"No couch," he murmured, his breath teasing her lips. And then he kissed her with such intensity she forgot where she was, why Luke was dangerous. She was shaking with desire and she could only wonder if her control wasn't a façade. Luke had seduced it from her.

Chapter Nine

Luke didn't take Julie to her place, as he'd initially said. He pulled into his parking lot instead and killed the engine.

"I thought we were going to my place?" she asked, a little too late at this point.

"Safer," he said. "And I doubt we'll see Blake tonight. He doesn't bring women to his place and Royce and Lauren are off to Hawaii."

He opened his door and slid out of the truck before she could say more. He'd decided well before the wedding ceremony that staying out of Julie's bed was an impossible undertaking. He wasn't, however, prepared to relinquish control to her. Allowing her to make their physical attraction a way to distance herself emotionally wasn't an option. His approach was everything and he knew it, or hell, maybe he was trying to justify his actions. He only knew that if he didn't manage the encounter just right, any hope he had of breaking down her walls would be destroyed the minute he slept with her.

He chose to bring her to his place: his home, his rules.

He needed the control with Julie.

Standing outside his apartment, he put the key in the lock. Anticipation thrummed through his veins. Damn if he wasn't getting hard just thinking about what was about to happen.

He pushed open his front door, but didn't move to enter his apartment. Instead, he turned to Julie, pulling her close. Brushing a lock of her hair from her cheek, he gave her a soft smile. Slowly, he lowered his head, bringing their lips close as he spoke, "I'm glad you're here."

He kissed her before she could respond, a slow, heated kiss full of invitation. He wanted her to let go and feel, to just be with him without any fears or walls.

Need heated his blood, burned a path through his veins, demanding and fierce, but still he held back, committed to his agenda. Julie was going to know this thing between them was more than sex; she was going to see, feel, and understand that he was in this for the finish line, that he intended to find out why he'd never forgotten her. Why no other woman compared.

Forcing himself to pull back from their kiss, he took her hand, leading her into his apartment before shutting the door behind them.

He flipped the hall light on, but no others. Despite her bold seductress persona, he knew he was going to test her, to push her, and somehow thought that tonight, she'd prefer the sanctuary of shadows. He planned to expose far more than her beautiful body before this evening ended.

She walked past him into his living room, the steady stream of moonlight glistening off her silky blonde hair, giving it a silvery quality. Her hips swayed in a slow, sultry motion as they strolled through his home, the only one he'd had in years, a place she felt right inside, just as she did by his side.

He let her explore, standing back and watching her as he loosened his tie and tossed it onto the hall table. He loosened the top buttons of his shirt at the same time he willed the urgency in his body to calm.

He wanted Julie like nothing else in this world, in a way he couldn't continue to ignore. He itched to peel off her dress, to once again touch that silky skin of hers. Patience, he reminded himself. Good things come to those who wait.

Slowly he walked into the living room, closing the distance between them, feeling like an animal stalking his prey, never taking his eyes off her. She picked up a picture of him and his brothers from the mantel. She stared at it a moment, and then looked up at him.

They stood a mere foot apart as their eyes locked. "I never knew you were so sentimental," she said in a soft voice.

He took the picture from her hands, setting it back on the mantel. "Runs in the family," he said as his hand settled on her hip. The air in the room seemed to crackle. "Sentimental and protective. You bring out those things and more in me. For instance, I remember every second of the weeks we spent together years ago, even when I tried to forget."

Her hand went to his jaw, tenderly, a soft look in her eyes. He pulled her close, tangling their legs together, melding his hips to hers, his thick erection to her stomach where she'd know just how hot he was for her.

Her teeth scraped her full bottom lip and his cock jerked. Damn, every time she did that he felt it in every inch of his body.

"How do I feel about it?" she asked softly.

"Mmmm," he said staring down at her, fighting the desire to just kiss her and ask questions later, when he knew it would be a fatal mistake.

Her dark lashes fluttered to her pale cheeks as if she was surrendering to some feeling. Her lips parted before she looked back up at him. "At this very moment, I'd say I feel pretty good about it."

She barely had the words out before his mouth was on hers, his tongue parting her lips, teasing and tasting, *and God*, she tasted good. Like chocolate and champagne, and temptation. The flavor sent a rush of blood through his veins that settled heavily, thickly in his groin.

His hands caressed a path down her waist, to cup her full, high, perfect ass. "I want to see you. All of you."

One side of her mouth lifted in a sultry little smile that played with his cock even as her fingers played with the buttons on his shirt. "And I want to see you."

He gently shackled her wrists with his hands, making her gaze lock with his. "You first. I want you way too much to be naked just yet, and way too much for you not to be."

Her eyes narrowed and he drew her wrist to his lips, feeling the thrum of her rapid pulse against his mouth before he moved to kiss her palm. "I'm, hmmmm, all for getting out of this dress."

His hands traveled down her neck, over her shoulders, and then gently over her breasts. She pressed his hands against her, molding them to her chest. "I need help with my zipper," she said. Slowly, she turned and gave him her back.

He brushed her hair over one of her delicate shoulders and tugged the metal clasp downward, each newly revealed inch of skin setting his pulse to a quicker pace. No woman had ever affected him so much with nothing but a slash of ivory skin. He kissed the sensitive spot at her nape and then slowly skimmed the material off her shoulders, then followed the dress down to her waist. She shimmied her hips, helping him pull it down until it pooled at her feet. His hands settled at her waist as she stepped aside and kicked away the garment.

She tried to rotate but he held her there. "Let me look at you," he said, sounding gruff, his voice thick with arousal. And look he did. Damn, the woman had a fine backside that the ivory thigh highs and strip of silk did everything to accent.

He popped the hook to her bra, and she shrugged it forward and tossed it to the floor. He stroked one lush butt cheek, and turned her to the fireplace. "Put your hands on the mantel," he ordered.

"Luke—"

He wrapped an arm around her waist and pressed his lips to her ear. "Tonight I'm in charge. Let me be in charge of your pleasure. You trust me enough to do what I say."

She rolled her head forward a moment, and while he could feel her resistance, he could also smell her arousal. He ran his hand over her breasts and then caressed one, teasing her nipple.

She moaned, and her head lifted and fell against his shoulder. "Put your hands on the mantel, sweetheart." He turned her toward the fireplace and held onto her while her hands curled around the ledge. Her silent submission, her willingness to trust him, held meaning he didn't miss, that he'd craved for far too long.

He didn't immediately let her go, sensing that she needed him to hold her, that she needed to go slow. He knew the implications of her letting go of her control. He knew how hard she clung to it. He even thought he was beginning to understand why. That she felt it made her stronger, that it kept her in control of life. Kept her from getting hurt.

He kissed her shoulder, trailing love bites, licks, and caresses down her arm, over her back, until he was on his knees, palms sliding down her thighs, then back up. His lips found the delicate skin of her backside, his hands pressed her legs apart, settling her the way he wanted her. The sight of her in panties, thigh highs and heels, and absolutely nothing else, was just a little piece of heaven.

He stroked between her thighs, beneath her panties, finding her slick and hot, the sounds of her moans making him hot. Yeah. Keeping his clothes on was smart, otherwise he might just stand up and bury himself exactly where he wanted to be – deep in the tight recesses of her perfect body. And she was perfect to him, the perfect woman in ways no other had ever been.

"Fuck me, Luke. Now," she murmured. "I want you."

He stilled.

Her words were like a slap. Reason told him it was just sex talk, but it wasn't enough. It pissed him off. He wanted 'make love to me.' She gave him 'fuck me'. Ironic really, since as a SEAL he'd always kept his relationships on the short term, no strings, no future 'fuck me' variety.

A surge of something he was pretty sure was anger blistered through him. He ripped her panties from her, then slid between her legs and rotated so that she stood in front of him, so that his mouth could come down on her clit with punishing pleasure. He lapped at her clit, the gasp she rewarded him with only driving that boiling feeling inside him. She wanted to be fucked, he'd fuck her all right. He'd fuck her like she'd never been fucked in her life.

He suckled her, drawing deeply on the swollen nub, delving two fingers inside her, caressing her. The taste of her arousal, the salty sweet flavor of woman, his woman who didn't know she was his, but he intended to show her, filled him. He intended to convince her. He felt it, *them*, their bond, and he wasn't going to let her run away.

Her fingers brushed through his hair, threaded through the strands and tugged almost roughly. His balls tightened and his dick stood at attention, stretching against his zipper. Still, he licked and teased and tested his own willpower until she gasped and her knees went weak. He wrapped his arm around her thighs, holding her up as he felt the ripples of release tighten on his fingers, reminding him of just how good it would be to bury himself inside the hot, tight enclave of her body. But there was still anger inside him, frustration and boiling hot emotion. Fuck me, she'd said.

Fuck me, he thought.

He eased her into a complete sated meltdown and picked her up, carrying her to an oversize leather lounge chair. He could feel her stare, but he didn't make eye contact. Not now, not this upset. But when he set her down, she pressed her lips to his and he found himself locked in a drugging kiss he didn't want. They'd kiss at the same time they went to his bedroom. When they made love.

She slid her hand over his crotch. He wanted her hand there but he pulled it away, his eyes meeting hers now. "Face the edge of the chair."

Uncertainty flared in her pretty blue eyes. "I can do much more facing you."

"And I can fuck you much better if you aren't. Turn over and let me look at you." He pressed her toward the end of the chair, leaned her over it, pulled her ass into the air and spread her wide. "You want to seduce me, you stay just like that while I undress, all wide open and ready for me." They'd delved into a bit of BDSM in the past and he used that now. He smacked her backside, just hard enough to remind her he was in charge.

She yelped and glanced over her shoulder and quickly. "That wasn't nice."

He smacked her again. "I'm not nice. Not when you don't do what I say."

"All right, Luke," she said softly. "But you better remember how good I am at this game."

"I remember how good you are at games, sweetheart," he promised. "I remember really damn well."

He pushed away from her and made quick work of undressing, sheathing the thick pulse of his erection with a condom he'd made sure was in his pocket before the wedding.

She didn't move. She just kept that fine ass in the air for him to drool over. He wasn't sure if that was good or bad. His cock didn't think it was bad, but then, he never seemed to think with the right head where Julie was concerned.

He moved to her, feeling like that wild animal again, framing her hips with his, his shaft settling between her legs. She moaned and arched towards him. He dragged his fingers through the wet heat of her sex, and then followed with his cock, before pressing inside her.

They moaned together at the first penetration, and he drove into her, until she had all of him. He fought the urge to lean in, to wrap himself around her and tell her what he felt, to tell her how much he'd craved this, and her. But he was human, and for the first time in a very long time, since the first time he'd been in a war zone and known he might have to pull the trigger – kill or be killed – he felt vulnerable.

He reached for the anger again, clung to it, and with it, pulled back and then pumped back into her. His hands settled on her slender backside, the sound of her moans ripping through him, driving him onward. He pumped and pumped, thrust, and ground into her. Faster and harder until their breathing filled his ears, and pleasure was all there was.

And somehow, he forgot the anger, somehow he wrapped himself around her, and was kissing her shoulder, her neck, whispering her name, touching her everywhere, anywhere. And he wanted to turn her over, he wanted to kiss her, to make love to her, but they were too far gone, too deep into each other, into the passion. He felt the rise of release in her, in him. Felt her body tense a moment before she clenched around his shaft, sending a rush of pleasure through him. His orgasm came with hers, hard and fast and unexpected, ripped from deep in his body.

When they both finally stilled, he collapsed gently around her, careful not to hurt her. He laid there for long moments, completely sated, blown away by how damn good sex was with Julie. Sex. God. He didn't know how he'd come to hate that word, when before Julie, he'd loved it so much.

Then, suddenly, he heard her muffled sobs. Crying. Julie, who put on this power chick facade, who made him believe she felt nothing, was crying. She'd buried her face in the chair, trying to muffle the sound, but she was absolutely crying. He'd done everything wrong with her, let emotion he wasn't used to experiencing drive his actions. And now he had to figure out how, and even if, he could fix this.

Chapter Ten

Julie tried to bite back her tears and failed. She had never been so confused and emotional in all her life. In fact, the past few days were all about confused. She was crying in front of Luke, or well, in his presence, and she really didn't want him to know.

He buried his face in her hair. "Don't cry." His voice was a gentle whisper against her neck. "Please baby, don't cry."

So much for hiding her face, so much for being the strong, in control woman, that she'd always been.

"Sweetheart, turn around," he urged, sliding away from her.

She turned all right, and tried to scoot off the chair before he saw her face, hoping for a mad dash for her clothes. No such luck. He tossed the condom in a trashcan and still managed to stop her progress, only to hug her and say, "I'm sorry."

He was sorry? Oh God. Now, she was so pathetic she'd made the man feel he had to apologize for having sex with her? She pushed back from him.

"There's nothing to be sorry for," she insisted, swiping at her damp cheeks, frustrated at herself for her weakness. "I'm hormonal, and my best friend got married, and my client might have killed his wife. I'm not myself. I just...I need to go home and have some time to myself." She tried to get up.

He stopped her again. "If you go home, I'm going with you."

She shook her head. "No." She crossed her arms over her chest, aware of her nakedness in a way she never had been before. And his. She was very aware of his long, lean, muscular body that she hadn't seen until now, because he put her back to him. "My building is safe. I have top notch security. I'll be fine."

"Your client might have killed his wife," he said. "You just said that yourself." He studied her for a long, intense moment. "You told me to fuck you and I got pissed about it."

The confession surprised her. "I...you used to like it when I said that."

"And I still would if the circumstances were different." He brushed the hair from her eyes. "I wanted tonight to be different. I..." He scrubbed his hand over his jaw and let out a heavy breath, leaning his elbows on his knees. "I screwed this up royally."

"You didn't screw up anything, Luke. I just don't know what you want from me."

He turned to her again. "What do you want from me?"

"I don't know," she said, feeling cornered and uncertain.

"You didn't complain when I brought you here tonight. You didn't argue when I said I was going to stay with you. What did you come here wanting tonight?"

She could say sex. She could, and she knew she could, and maybe she even should. But she didn't. She reached up and ran her fingers over the strong line of his jaw and she said exactly what she felt. "I just wanted to be with you."

His eyes settled heavily on her face, a muscle in his jaw flexing. "You wanted sex."

"No," she said quickly. "I mean yes. No. I just wanted to be with you, Luke, and if that's the wrong—"

He picked her up and she yelped at the sudden action, clinging to him until they were off the main living room and inside the master suite.

Unlike Lauren and Royce's place, there a huge window above a massive bed, where moonlight beamed down and illuminated the room. He laid her on the bed and settled his big, wonderful, naked body on top of hers.

"Do you know what I wanted when I brought you here tonight?"

There was something in his eyes that made her heart thunder in her ears and her chest tighten. "What?"

"To make love to you, Julie," he said. "To have you make love to me. And I didn't think that's what you wanted at all."

That tight feeling in her chest expanded and her eyes began to burn again. He was asking her to give them a chance beyond sex and while she knew this was the moment of no return she really should run from, she couldn't. She wrapped her arms around his neck. "I'd like that very much."

With those words, there was a dangerously scary and somehow remarkably wonderful crack in her armor that became even more wonderful when he kissed her, when he made love to her with that kiss. But when he was inside her again, when they moved together, when she stared into his eyes, she felt no fear. There was nothing left but Luke and endless possibility.

***

Julie woke in a dark, dark place. She tried to move, but her shoulders were lodged against something. She reached up with her hands and hit something solid. Oh God. Where was she? Hello! Hello! She tried to move again, and panic rose inside her. She started pushing on the hard surface over her head. It was too dark, way too dark. Suffocating. She coughed, realizing she couldn't breathe and suddenly it was hot. So very hot. Orange light flamed around her and she could see now. She was in a casket. The wood around her began to burn, flames licking at her limbs.

Julie sat up and gasped for air, running her hands over her arms, her breath heaving out. She was not burning. She was not in a casket.

Luke was beside her, saying something. "Julie. Baby. It was a dream."

She blinked into the sunlight, bringing a massive Ansel Adams black and white woodsy scene into focus. It hung on the wall in front of Luke's bed.

90

"Nightmare," she whispered, and turned to him. "Luke, I was in a casket going up in flames, and," she swallowed hard, "I'm sure you know where this is going. I need to call her sister."

"Then we'll call," he assured her and reached over her to pull open a black nightstand where he removed the piece of paper. "I'll get you a phone."

"I left mine in your truck, I think," she said. "I don't remember bringing in my purse at all."

He brushed his lips over hers. "I'll go get it, but I'd rather you call from mine. Just to be safe, in case the line is tapped by someone other than Blake. No sense in making it easy on them to get your address."

A few minutes later, Julie was wearing Luke's shirt, standing in his kitchen waiting on the coffee she'd made to finish brewing, and feeling a little shy about the night before. Shy. Her. Go figure. Lauren would never believe it. *She* could hardly believe it. She was falling for Luke in a big way. Heck, who was she kidding? She'd fallen big years ago and she was just falling deeper now.

"Hope you made enough for me," he said from behind her.

She glanced over her shoulder, and found herself breathless at the sight he made, standing there holding her purse. She turned to inspect him, taking in the jeans and a t-shirt he'd haphazardly pulled on, looking as delicious as he did in a suit or tuxedo. With his dark hair rumpled from sleep and her fingers and sporting a seriously sexy one day shadow on his jaw, he definitely gave new meaning to good morning.

"Your purse is supposed to match the outfit," she teased.

"I've never been much on matching outfits," he said, setting it down on the table top and then sitting down.

She filled two mugs and grabbed spoons before joining him. The cream and sugar were already on the table. "Since you got my purse for me, I made enough for you, too."

"Well then," he said, doctoring his coffee with lots of cream. "I'll have to find a new strategy tomorrow, I guess."

"Who says I'll be here tomorrow?" she challenged, warmed by the idea that she would be.

"Danger's in the air," he said. "And even if it weren't true, and it is, I'd use whatever excuse I had to in order to keep you here."

"I think...I'd let you."

A slow smile turned up the corners of his mouth. "Good to know." He motioned to the other room. "Let's go to my office. I want you to call from my land line and I'll have the cordless. Say as little as possible and agree to nothing I don't give a nod of approval to."

"Okay," she said, and rose.

Luke's office was lined with framed Sports Illustrated magazine covers that spanned years. He was clearly a collector. But then, he loved sports, especially baseball. She sat down behind his desk, letting the plush leather chair soothe the stiffness in her body.

"Her name is Diana," Luke said, resting a hip on the desk. "And according to the official reports, there's been no dispute of the suicide and there is no criminal investigation."

She nodded and took the phone, feeling as nervous as the day she'd taken the bar exam.

"Don't agree to anything unless I give you a nod," he reminded her.

She nodded. "What's the number?"

He arched a brow. "No argument?"

"Part of doing my job well is being smart enough to call on experts when I need to, and actually listen when they talk. In this case, you're my expert."

Surprise flickered on his face before he read off the number from memory and then put the receiver in his hand to his ear.

"Hello," a female voice said on the second ring. The sound of her voice was so familiar, so Elizabeth, that Julie's stomach knotted.

Julie discreetly cleared her suddenly parched throat. "Hello, this is Julie Harrison."

"Oh, thank God," the woman said. "I'm not sure this line is safe. Meet me in an hour at the dinosaur display in the Metropolitan Museum."

Julie's eyes went to Luke's. "But-"

The line went dead.

Luke cursed under his breath. "This could be a setup. You realize that, right?"

She nodded in agreement and pushed to her feet before wrapping her arms around his neck. "Which is why I'm glad I have a big, bad ass, ex-Navy SEAL bodyguard. And in order to save time, I think we should share the shower at my place so I can change."

***

They were ten minutes late. Julie eyed her watch with concern as she and Luke stepped through the doors of the museum, cold air chasing them through the entry. She shivered and tugged her leather jacket closer, thankful she'd stopped by home to change into black wool pants and a black sweater. That bridesmaid's dress would have made the cold day even colder.

Luke stood beside her, dressed in jeans, a sweater, and a leather jacket. They scanned the magnificent room with sky high ceilings, and though he might appear relaxed, she could feel the tension rippling off of him. He was not happy about this meeting.

A guard walked up to Julie and handed her an envelope. She tore it open immediately and showed it to Luke. "She says to meet her at the dinosaurs. I guess that means we need tickets."

"Tickets it is," he said, drawing her hand in his. "I'm keeping you close. It's safer that way."

"That's not how it worked out in the shower, thus why we're late."

"I behave in public," he assured her. "Mostly."

She laughed, which was remarkable considering her nerves were prickling with so much force that she had to fight the urge to rub her hands up and down her arms. She was used to the adrenaline of negotiations, but this was different. This was darker, and she wondered how Lauren had dealt with the viciousness of the crimes she often took to trial.

Once they had their tickets and reached the fifth floor, they walked to the middle of the dinosaur display. Looking around, Julie sighed. "The whole floor is part of the display. Do you suppose she plans to find us?"

He shrugged. "I would assume that's the idea. Let's step to a quiet corner where she won't feel intimidated."

"The bench over there." Julie pointed to a corner with an empty sitting area. "You don't think she'll be afraid to approach me with you here do you?"

"It didn't bother her the first time," he reminded her, as they headed to the spot she'd indicated and took a seat.

Luke had hardly said the words, when a woman wearing dark glasses and a scarf over her hair approached.

"Thank you for coming." She glanced between them, removing her sunglasses. "Both of you. I'm Diana Macom, which is Elizabeth's maiden name, but I'm sure you know that by now."

The woman's eyes, so like Elizabeth's, reached into Julie's soul and twisted.

"The coffee shop is busier than I'd like," she said. "Maybe we should stay here."

Luke stood up to let her sit and then squatted beside them and Julie knew it was because he was watching her and not just listening to her. Diana removed her glasses. "I'm sure you've figured out I'm Elizabeth's sister, by now."

"That's hard to miss," Julie commented. "You're so alike." Julie decided an introduction was in order. "This is—"

"Luke Walker, I know," she said. "I checked into private investigators. The Walker brothers have a reputation."

Luke's face was unreadable. "Then you know we do mostly airport and corporate security work."

"I know you're all capable of doing whatever you want to do and well," she said, and pulled a small journal from her purse. "She wrote about you."

The hair on Julie's nape lifted. "That's...Elizabeth's?"

"Yes." Her voice hitched and she swallowed hard. "She wrote about a lot of things she didn't dare say out loud." Her spine stiffened. "My sister did not kill herself."

"The police say she did," Luke countered, though his tone was gentle.

"They're wrong," Diana bit out with no gentleness in return. "Judge Moore is very influential. Of course, Elizabeth's death wasn't deemed suspicious. Who would cross the man? I need help from someone who isn't influenced by him or afraid of him."

"You think he killed her?" Julie asked in a low voice.

Diana's lips tightened. "Read that journal and then you tell me. If not him, then someone connected to him. Someone close. The question is, how close?" She paused. "There's so much damning information in that journal and people are named."

"Did she tell you about any of this?" Luke asked. "Or did you just read about it?"

"She didn't tell me," she said. "In fact, she said the farther I stayed from her husband the happier she'd be." She inhaled and let it out, seeming to fight tears. "I've tried to piece together the tidbits in the journal. I'm fairly certain that the Judge is involved in something dirty and that he and another high-level official of some sort double-crossed whoever they've been working for."

"Why come to Julie over this?" Luke asked. "Why not contact Elizabeth's attorney?"

"Because we both thought he was being paid under the table by the judge," Diana said flatly.

"But Julie worked for the judge," Luke argued.

"Her best friend is a former Assistant District Attorney, who is connected to any number of trust-worthy people, or organizations, including Walker Security," she said, and glanced at Julie. "And because Elizabeth met you and told me that she believed you had no idea what you were involved in."

"Yet she didn't tell you what she was involved in?" Julie queried.

Her lips thinned. "No. And believe me, I tried to pull it out of her. Look. All I'm asking is for you both to read the journal, and if you see what I do, and I know you will, then please help me get justice for my sister." She held up the journal. "I'll pay the Walker rate. Elizabeth had life insurance and I was the beneficiary. There is no better way to spend that money than to let her rest in peace knowing her killer, or killers, are brought to justice."

Julie's eyes met Luke's, giving him a pleading look.

Luke let out a resigned sigh and accepted the journal. "We'll look this over and get back with you."

Chapter Eleven

It was late afternoon by the time Luke sat on Julie's couch reading the journal, with Cici, the ever-friendly feline, purring and brushing back and forth against his leg. With her stockinged feet tucked under her, Julie was glued to his side, trying not to miss a word. A guy could get used to having Julie this close and this involved in what he was doing.

"Wait," she said as he started to turn the page. "I'm not done yet."

He arched a brow at her slow perusal of the material.

She gave him a disapproving look with those gorgeous blue eyes. "You might miss something reading so fast."

"This isn't a contract," he reminded her. "It's a woman's thoughts. Some of which are none of our business."

Julie leaned back against the couch cushions as she considered his words. "I know. It is kind of creepy reading a dead woman's journal, isn't it?"

"Very." Luke set the journal on the coffee table in front of him. "I don't like this entire situation. Most importantly, I don't like you involved."

"I don't like me involved," she agreed. "But I am and we can't change that."

He studied her a long moment, saw the pink flush of her cheeks, read the guilt she felt over Elizabeth and didn't deserve. "You're involved because the judge and Elizabeth both pulled you into this. Not because of some sort of responsibility."

"Yes," she insisted. "There is responsibility for me in this." He started to object and she held up a hand. "Please hear me out. I know you're trying to protect me, Luke. I appreciate it, probably a whole lot more than you understand. But there's

97

right and wrong in life, and I try to do right. Doing something about this is the right thing to do."

Luke leaned back next to her and turned to face her, falling harder every time he got a glimpse of who she was as a person. "I understand."

"You do?"

"Yes," he said, stroking her cheek. "We have to look into this, and we have to decide if, and when, to go to the police. And yes, it's the right thing to do."

"What if someone on the police force is involved in this?"

"We don't even know what 'this' is or isn't, at this point. Let's not assume anyone is corrupt."

"Come on, Luke," she pressed. "You read what I did in that journal. That man Elizabeth wrote about, what was his name," she paused and snapped her fingers, "Paul Arel. That's it. And then someone called 'Dragonfly'. Clearly, that's a code name. It sounds like the judge and that Dragonfly person were doing deals behind Arel's back. And then there's the stolen artwork. The journal says it's hidden behind a wall in the study."

"We don't know if it's true or who the real players are," he countered. "Give me time to investigate. And for all we know Paul Arel is a code name as well."

"What if Elizabeth's threat related to Dragonfly? Maybe the judge didn't want her to tell him he was being cheated."

"Dragonfly could be a man or woman," he reminded her. "It could even be Elizabeth's sister, and she could be setting us up."

She sat up. "Surely not? Do you think that is possible?"

"Everything is possible." Hell, he'd seen SEALs he'd have believed to be unbreakable cry under imminent threat of capture.

"I should know that," she said tightly. "The judge alone should have been a wake-up call, if not the very dark side I see divorce bring out in people."

There was that cynical part of her that kept the wall wedged between them. "Lauren mentioned you were thinking of leaving your firm, and maybe doing something other than divorce cases?"

"Not really," she said thoughtfully. "I mean, yes, I've given it consideration, and at times, fairly seriously. In the end though, I'm making money that I can set aside, and I'm secure. I can't lose that."

Because she felt alone. He knew it, but he didn't say it. Putting her on the defensive was a move that hadn't worked well for him thus far. "You never see your father?"

She chewed her bottom lip and cut her gaze. "Not since I was a child."

"And you don't want to see your mother?" he asked, recalling the past talks they'd had, back when she thought he'd be gone and her confessions wouldn't matter.

She shrugged and hugged her knees to her chest. "I never know where she is. Vegas, or off traveling with some new man or husband."

"She still performs?"

She nodded. "She's still gorgeous, even in her forties. She had me when she was only eighteen and I think she resented being held back, but then, she never really was."

"Do you talk on the holidays?"

"We talk on Christmas and occasionally on Thanksgiving."

Not her birthday, he thought. Not in person. "When was the last time you saw her?"

"Her and her new man stopped by three years ago. He hit on me and suggested a threesome."

"What?" he asked, astonished. "With your mother?"

"Sick, right?"

"And your mother said?"

"She's a prim and proper princess. She doesn't do those things."

Luke sat there a moment, speechless. When he recovered, he turned her so that she faced him, his hands on her knees. "Let's make a pact right now."

"What kind of pact?"

"No matter what happens to us, we are friends, and you are a part of the Walker family. Nothing is going to keep you from Lauren, or from us. You understand?"

Her eyes immediately glossed over with tears. "Luke-"

He brushed his lips over hers. "I'm serious, Julie. No matter what, you have me." He wiped a tear as it escaped down her cheek. "Let's get Cici and your stuff and go to my place where I know you're safe."

"You want to take Cici with us?"

"She's your family," he said. "So yes. I want to take Cici."

"That means a litter box," she reminded him.

"You mean she isn't toilet trained?"

She laughed. "Oh how I wish."

She wasn't arguing and that said she was really rattled, or he was getting through to her. Or maybe, just maybe, it was both. Either way, Luke was getting them out of here before she changed her mind. Because not only was he feeling the very male need to have her in his bed, he was far more disturbed by that journal than he'd let on.

***

She'd grocery shopped with Luke.

Julie stood in his kitchen, in soft cotton pink sweats, a Victoria Secrets 'Pink ' T-shirt, and fuzzy pink slippers, dicing tomatoes for a salad. She was out of her personal space, her zone, and yet she felt oddly at peace.

Julie cut her gaze to the side and smiled as she watched Luke stirring the spaghetti sauce barely a foot away from her, throwing in various spices here and there as if it were a science. She decided right then that there was something about a man who could handle a gun and a spatula.

Looking down as she heard a soft purr Julie realized that Cici was once again wrapping herself around Luke's feet, but he didn't seem to mind so she didn't say anything. The cat loved

Luke. Her chest tightened. Love. God. Was she falling in love with Luke? Had she already?

He tasted the sauce. "Love it."

"What?" Julie asked, jolted by his words.

"The sauce is exactly the way my mother makes it," he said.

"Oh," she said, sighing in relief. "And you only had to call her three times."

He grinned. He was so handsome when he grinned like that. "She loves it when I call her."

"She was in a movie."

He shrugged. "She didn't mind."

She arched a brow. "You mean you didn't mind interrupting her date."

"If he can't take the good with the bad, he shouldn't be around."

"That's evil, Luke."

"Testing his patience is part of being sure he's in this for the long haul."

She shook her head and resumed chopping. "Dating is hard enough, Luke."

"Says you?" he asked.

"Says everyone," she said flatly. "Which is why I don't do it."

"What do you mean exactly by that?"

She flicked him a quick glance, and shrugged. "I just don't do it."

"At all?"

She didn't look at him. "That pretty much sums it up."

He couldn't help asking, "What about sex?"

She stopped chopping. "What about it?"

He gave her a knowing look. "You like it."

She laughed, but without humor. "So do you."

"You're avoiding the question."

She started chopping again. "What was the question?"

"If you don't date, what do you do about sex?"

"Not much since you left," she said, so appalled she'd admitted that that her hand slipped on the knife handle, and she cut her finger. Blood immediately poured from the sliced skin. "Ouch." She rushed her hand to the sink.

Luke grabbed her wrist and turned on the water. "It looks pretty deep."

"Fingers bleed a lot and I'm fine, really."

He turned off the water. "We need to bandage it." He pulled her gently along until they reached the bathroom and ordered, "Sit and hold the towel snug until I get the supplies."

She did as he instructed as he rummaged through the medicine chest and pulled out what he wanted. Kneeling at her feet he checked the cut. "A little deeper and you would have needed stitches for sure, but I think you'll manage to skate by without them."

"Good," she said. "An evening in the ER would not be fun." Would he have gone with her? Had she ever had anyone but Lauren who would have? She watched him doctoring her finger, thinking about how different he was or maybe how different she was because of him. When he'd almost finished, she reached out and threaded her fingers through the silky black strands of his hair. "Thank you for taking care of me."

He stopped working, studying her with such intensity she felt like he could see clear to her soul. She wanted to look away, and yet she didn't.

"Someone has to," he said finally.

His words warmed her, thrilled her, and she fought to remember why Luke taking care of her was a bad thing. To say that she felt confused was an understatement.

"I get by on my own pretty well, but still, it's nice to have you help me tonight."

"If tonight is all you'll give me," he said after a long pause, "it's a start and I'll take it."

A funny feeling fluttered in her chest, an emotion she didn't want to deal with. She leaned forward and pressed her mouth to his. They lingered there until his hand lifted and curled around her neck, his tongue caressing hers. Heat pooled low in her stomach, and that funny feeling in her chest expanded when she'd thought it would go away.

"I want you," she whispered against his lips. "I want to touch you, Luke." She tugged on his shirt with her good hand. "And see you."

He pulled back and regarded her with a heavy-lidded stare so intense she couldn't breathe. When he moved, she thought he might get up, might refuse her, but instead he tossed his shirt away. Then suddenly this powerful, sexy man was undressing her, and instead of sex making her feel just as powerful, in control, she felt fragile. Only fragile didn't feel bad. It felt good. It felt like she didn't have to try, she didn't have to do anything but just be with him, relax and enjoy every kiss, every taste, every touch. But what if she gave everything she was, and then there was nothing left? Was it already too late? Maybe she already had.

***

After hours of talking, and making love, and making love some more, Julie and Luke were starving, and since he'd burned the sauce, they ordered pizza.

Julie lounged against his headboard, wearing only his t-shirt, while he wore the low-slung jeans he'd pulled on to greet the delivery man. As she was as big a sports fan as Luke, they'd eaten a large pizza while watching SportsCenter and arguing about baseball pitchers.

They were fighting over the last slice when Luke's cell phone rang by the nightstand. He reached over her and kissed her before snagging it. His brow furrowed at the number, and then he answered, "This is Luke Walker."

Julie watched his emotionless face as he listened, and then said, "I'm still considering it." He listened a minute longer and then hung up without saying another word.

"Something wrong?" she asked, fairly certain that answer was 'yes'. Luke might not have reacted to the call, but his lack of reaction in itself was telling.

"That was Elizabeth's sister," he surprised her by saying. "She was following up to see if we'd made a decision about helping or not."

"That was fast," Julie said. "It's barely a full day."

"And she called me, not you."

"I noticed that," she said. "Not that she had my number. Makes me wonder if she was using me to get to you."

"You know what I wonder?" he asked but didn't wait for a reply. "I wonder how she got my number when it's a private line I don't give out freely."

Chapter Twelve

Monday morning, after Luke insisted on dropping her off, Julie headed up the steps in her office building with her cream colored heels clicking on the pavement. Protective as he was, she should feel suffocated, but she didn't. Maybe it was how great the weekend with him had been, or maybe it was the nightmares about Elizabeth that continued to haunt her.

She turned to wave to him where he waited by the curb and then headed into the building. With a smile, she refocused on the glass doors, catching a glimpse of herself in a light blue suit dress. The reflection of a man drew her up short.

She froze, then frowned. The image had disappeared. It couldn't have been who she'd thought it was. It was so ridiculous that she wasn't even going to let herself finish the thought. She forced herself not to turn around again and to head into the building for fear of alarming Luke, but as she walked across the glossy white lobby floor she was more bothered than not. The thought she didn't let herself finish came to her mind of its own accord.

The reflection had been of a man who looked just like the stranger from the Chicago hotel, the one from the elevator and the bar. Which again, she thought, was insanity. Julie waved at the security guard sitting at the long black glass panel, and headed for the elevator.

She stepped into the quiet lobby of the law firm she had considered her second home for years. Once she was in the private office area she found her secretary, Gina, already sitting at her desk working.

"Morning," Gina said, her auburn hair twisted elegantly at her nape, her olive green suit matching her eyes perfectly. "Coffee's ready. I'll bring a cup in to you."

Julie stopped in front of Gina's desk. She was pretty and efficient, and even played cat sitter for Julie on this last trip, and yet Julie barely knew her. She didn't let herself get close to people at work. She didn't let herself get close to anyone but Lauren and...Luke.

"That's thoughtful," Julie said. "Thank you. I'm not sure I say that enough."

Gina blinked and a stunned look slid over her face. "I've been bringing you coffee for as long as I've been here, and you have, uh, never said anything like that."

Julie silently replayed Gina's words in her head. Anything like that. Surely she didn't mean 'thank you'. When had she become that uncaring of others? Had she survived this life, this world of divorce, by blocking out the rest of the world to the point she didn't even behave politely?

"Well," Julie said slowly. "I should have. I'm really sorry." Julie left Gina gaping at her, and the reaction twisted her in knots. She wasn't liking the view of herself from her assistant's eyes. She'd had to withdraw to survive her career, and it had changed her.

Julie walked into her office without another word. She deposited her briefcase on the credenza and her purse in a drawer before sitting down behind her desk. Dropping her elbows on the flat surface, she let her chin settle on her knuckles.

Julie's cell phone rang and she answered it without looking at the caller. "Did you read it?"

Spine stiffening, Julie recognized the voice, so like Elizabeth's, "Diana," she said, surprised, not wanting to say too much, too soon. "I'm working on it, but reading someone's personal journal is rather disconcerting."

"I know," she said. "But please read it. There are things in it that will change how you feel about her death, I promise you."

"Okay, yes."

"Thank you, Ms. Harrison. Thank you." She hung up.

Julie looked up to find Gina standing in the doorway. "I didn't want to interrupt. I have your coffee."

"Yes please. Thank you."

Gina set a cup of coffee in front of Julie. "Why are you a paralegal instead of an attorney?" Julie asked her.

Surprise registered in Gina's expression. "It wasn't by choice. It just sort of happened."

Julie's eyes narrowed. "Meaning?"

"Life, finances, a sick parent. All those things combined kept me from achieving all of my goals."

Julie's eyes dropped to her desk. She had worked herself through school, so she understood struggling. She just had never tried to understand Gina's. Maybe she could help her finish school.

Impulsively, Julie looked at Gina and asked, "Would you like to go to lunch today?"

"Ah," Gina paused as if she couldn't figure out how to respond and then suddenly smiled. "Sure."

"Excellent," Julie said. "I'm looking forward to it."

The phone in the lobby buzzed. "I better get that," Gina said, and rushed away.

The next few hours went by quickly, and not without a number of distracted thoughts of Luke, and a text message to check on her. She'd liked that message, too, far more than she would have ever expected.

It was close to lunchtime when Gina buzzed Julie's office again. "Judge Moore is here to see you."

Julie drew back in surprise. "I wasn't expecting him, but...yes. Okay. Send him in."

Dropping her pen onto the desk, Julie leaned back in her chair, resting her elbows on the arms. She had no desire to stand and greet the judge, regardless of the fact he deserved the respect if she was to keep him a courtroom ally.

Her office door opened and Gina poked her head in. Waving the judge forward, she offered him coffee and he refused. Good, Julie thought, he won't be staying long.

The judge appeared in her doorway. "Julie," he said with a nod, looking his normal proper self, in a blue suit that was custom-fitted to his trim fifty-something physique, his gray hair neatly trimmed.

"Judge," she greeted.

Clearly taking the greeting as an invitation, in several long strides, the judge stood in front of Julie's desk. Usually she would have moved to the conference table in the corner of her room. No doubt, he noticed that today she did no such thing.

He gave her an assessing stare, letting her know that *yes* he noticed, before sitting in a visitor's chair.

"I'm sorry about Elizabeth," she said when he didn't immediately speak.

His expression was respectfully grim, his eyes surprisingly direct as they met hers. "As am I."

"I was shocked," she said, awkwardness expanding in the room.

"Yes," he agreed. "I was as well. I had no idea she had taken this all so hard." He sighed. "Obviously, I won't need your services. That is, unless her family causes trouble over our assets."

Julie went cold. She had a bad feeling this visit had a hidden purpose. "Do you expect them to?"

He ran his hand over the back of his neck as if all the tension in the room had settled there. "I doubt it, but the quicker I get this behind me the better. It's hard enough – divorce, that is – without this turn of events."

How hard was it, she wondered? "I assume there are no documents or will that I need to know about other than what I'm aware of?"

"She had life insurance," he said. "I have no idea if it was left to me or her sister at this juncture of our relationship."

"Sister?" Julie asked in a voice that was a bit too high.

"Her twin. Never did like me. She was always trying to get Elizabeth to leave me."

"Considering that's what you wanted, I would think you would like her."

He shrugged. "I preferred to do the leaving on my terms."

As do most rich men who want to shuffle their assets, but Julie didn't say that.

He made a disgusted sound. "Believe me, Diana – that's Elizabeth's sister – is trouble. She only wanted her to leave me to take my money. If she can get an attorney to take the case, she'll fight for some of it now. The life insurance won't be enough for her. She's a greedy little bitch." He waved a dismissive hand. "There's another reason I came by. You've handled a number of children's charity functions and I know they're dear to your heart. Elizabeth was in charge of a Children's Cancer Association function tomorrow night and my artwork will be on display. I must admit I wish it wasn't this week, but it was impossible to cancel with such advanced planning. I'd appreciate it if you would consider playing hostess in her absence."

She hesitated. Because of the judge's involvement, she was almost certain she could hear Luke warning her away from the man. But she couldn't. Not when it came to this. "Of course," Julie said. "It is, as always, kind of you to show your art for such good causes. Can you send me the details so I know what I need to do?"

"My secretary will email them within the hour," he said and stood. They said their goodbyes and Julie watched him leave. Why did she feel so out of sorts, like she'd been set up?

She tried to dial Luke, but he didn't answer. She felt uncomfortable leaving the building today. She didn't want to cancel lunch with Gina, but maybe they could order in and talk. She headed to the lobby to find out.

"How would you feel about Chinese?" Julie asked Gina as she came up behind her.

Gina jumped. "Oh, you scared me." She shuffled a few papers and quickly shut a file as she swiveled her chair around to face her boss. "I guess I'm wrapped a little tightly today."

Julie smiled. "Sorry about that. I don't blame you for being jumpy. It's not every day a woman walks into our offices and then dies days later."

Gina shoved her hair out of her eyes. "I must admit it's a bit creepy. If I were one of the family members, I'd be asking questions about her death."

"Did you know she had a twin sister?" Julie asked, leaning a hip on the desk, and wondering just what Elizabeth might have chatted about in the lobby the day of her visit.

"Really? I had no idea."

"Neither did I until she walked up to me at the the funeral," Julie said. "Talk about making someone jump. It was like seeing a ghost."

The buzzer on Gina's desk went off, ringing from the main reception area on the floor above theirs that handled ten attorneys. "There is a man here to see Julie, a Luke Walker. I sent him to your floor a few minutes ago. Sorry. Would have called sooner but I got busy."

The elevator dinged just beyond the lobby and Julie stood up and smoothed a hand over her dress, willing the butterflies in her stomach that no man had ever given her before, to calm down.

Gina arched a brow. "Someone good, I hope?"

Luke ambled into the room, tall and lean in a pair of black jeans, a black t-shirt and a leather jacket, looking as predatory as a panther on the prowl. The instant his eyes touched Julie, sweeping her from head to toe, it was clear she was that prey.

"Yes," Gina whispered. "Someone good for sure."

Yes indeed, Julie thought. She never got over the impact he made on her when he entered a room. "I hope this is a good news visit." Like Elizabeth wasn't murdered and all her paranoia wasn't merited.

"It is if you're hungry," he said, giving Gina a polite nod and then fixing Julie with a hot stare from which it was impossible to misread the personal nature of their relationship. "I was hoping to steal you away for lunch."

Oh how she wanted to have lunch with Luke, or better yet, have Luke for lunch, but she wasn't going to forget Gina. Not this time. Not again.

"Actually," she said, hating how hoarse her voice sounded, how easily he affected her, and how good he smelled, "My assistant, Gina, and I planned to have lunch today."

"I need to cancel anyway," Gina said quickly, but she didn't look at Julie. "I forgot I have to run an errand at lunch."

"Luke could join us for lunch and then you could run your errand on the way back," she offered.

Gina gave Julie a smile that didn't quite meet her eyes. "This is going to take a while," she said. "It just came up and it's pretty important. Would you mind if I was a little late returning?"

"No, of course not, there isn't anything pressing going on today. Maybe tomorrow we could try again. You know, for lunch?"

"Sure," Gina said and turned back to her desk.

Julie frowned, feeling oddly uneasy with what had just transpired for no identifiable reason other than a shade of guilt because she really wanted to be alone with Luke.

Luke settled his hand on her back. "Can you leave now?"

Julie looked up into his warm brown eyes and almost sighed. Looking into his eyes was like flipping some switch inside her to the on position.

"Yes. Be right back." She turned, a niggling feeling of unease in her gut she couldn't put aside, even for the hot man in the lobby. She returned quickly with her coat on and her purse over her shoulder but paused at the door when she found Luke leaning against the wall by Gina's desk, making small talk. Julie could just see Gina, and she wasn't making direct eye contact with Luke any more than she had Julie. She seemed nervous, even uncomfortable, under his inspection.

"I'm ready," Julie said, stepping to his side and then telling Gina, "Just forward the phones upstairs and lock up." She'd eagerly volunteered to move to a separate floor, leaving some of the firm's politics behind when space had become an issue for the firm.

The instant Julie and Luke stepped onto the otherwise empty elevator he pulled her close and kissed her, but any thrill she got from it, which was plenty, faded as he warned, "Be careful what you say around her."

"Why?"

"She hates you and I don't trust her."

Julie drew back in shock. "What?"

"It's in her eyes when she looks at you, and she wouldn't look me in the eye. I never like that."

Julie hugged herself, feeling his words like a blade. The elevator dinged and people got in. She stepped away from Luke, to remain professional, and to get some much needed space. She didn't look at him but she could feel him watching her, willing her to.

"How about the Mexican joint on the corner?" he asked when they stepped into the main lobby.

"Yes, sure," she said, tying her coat closed.

The wind gusted around them as they headed down the steps, chilly but not freezing, though she was feeling pretty darn cold.

"I upset you," Luke said as they turned right on the sidewalk.

She cast him a sideways look. "You were just being honest and I prefer honesty, even when it's hard to swallow."

They passed a vacant shop, and Luke pulled her into the nook, out of sight, and wrapped her in his powerful arms, the heat of his body seeping into hers.

"I'm sorry," he said, brushing hair from her face. "I shouldn't have said that about Gina so abruptly. I'm feeling protective. The Walker men seem to be genetically programmed to get that way with our women."

"Your women?" she asked, surprised by the comment.

"Yeah," he said, lowering his mouth, his lips all but brushing hers. "My woman." He slanted his mouth over hers and claimed it with a hot kiss that stole her breath, before asking, "You got something to say about that?"

"Maybe," she said.

"Maybe?"

She leaned back, hands on his chest. "This thing with Gina is bothering me, Luke. It's...I honestly stay so detached at work that I focused on how good she is at her job, not personal likes or dislikes, which suddenly feels very shallow of me." Just like so many of her clients.

He studied her a long moment. "If anyone understands what it's like to lock your emotions away so that you get the job done, I do."

But he'd been a soldier, in war. This wasn't what a person's job was supposed to make them. She didn't recognize herself. She didn't understand what was happening to her, and she wasn't sure she could with Luke in her life, not when he took it over as he did. Maybe he was even the reason she was such a mess.

"I'm not hungry. I need to get some work done." She pushed away from him and to her surprise, he let her. Julie walked away from him, feeling alone. Alone was familiar, and she tried to embrace it. Alone meant standing on her own two feet, that she would take actions to protect herself, never getting caught off guard. Alone meant she never had to walk away and be so ridiculously conflicted that she wanted someone – Luke – to pull her back, only to be disappointed when it didn't happen.

***

Gina ordered a sandwich at the nearby deli and waited patiently at the take out counter. It didn't surprise her that Julie had backed out of lunch. People like Julie always thought they were above people like her. She didn't know much about Julie's past, since Julie didn't talk to her about anything, but she imagined her boss must have been born with a silver spoon in her mouth. After all, she was extremely young to have achieved such success.

Gina hated her.

If things had been different it would have been her who had such success. The fake niceness Julie had handed out today sickened her. Damn good thing lunch had been cancelled. She wouldn't want to be sick at the table, and eating with Julie might just have done that to her.

When her food was ready, she accepted her take-out bag. Thoughts of Julie's demise made her strides towards the door a bit more energetic. Shoving it open, she stepped outside and quickly turned the corner. She came to an abrupt halt as she ran smack into a very hard something.

Her balance faltered and strong hands steadied her. "Easy now, bébé."

Something about the French accent insinuated itself into her senses like a soft breeze, caressing her nerve endings into awareness. She looked up into sky blue eyes that were alive with interest.

"Sorry about that," she said.

The man was tall, with brownish blond hair that was a little too long. His body was Adonis-like, his smile sexy as hell. "Perhaps is fate, no?"

She tilted her head. This guy made her heart go pitter patter with a whole new tune. And that accent… "Perhaps, yes."

He reached his arm overhead flattening his palm on the wall to support his weight. His eyes grazed her lips and lingered before settling back on her eyes. "I am Marco."

She wet her lips and then offered him her free hand. "I'm Gina."

He brought her knuckles to his lips and kissed them. "A pleasure, cherie. I think we should take advantage of this chance meeting. When can I see you again?"

Gina wanted this man. He absolutely made her burn. The gods above seemed to have presented her with her own special sex toy. "Dinner. Tonight. My place."

He smiled, his eyes reflecting his approval. Her gaze traveled down his body, to his belt, and below. He was hard. She stared a moment, not afraid of the boldness it represented. Then she looked up at him, and smiled her favorite wicked smile. "Tonight indeed. Got a pen? I wouldn't want you getting lost or anything."

There was a glint of something she didn't quite understand in his eyes as he reached forward and ran a finger down her cheek. "I never get lost, so, ma cherie, plan on being found. " He keyed her address in his cell phone and she sighed as he sauntered away. Once he was out of sight, she headed to her apartment to take her long lunch and break out some sexy lingerie.

***

A half hour after Julie had left Luke on the corner, she sat at her desk, her stomach growling, thumbing through a case file and the silence was deafening to the point of creepy. The creek of the wooden floor in the lobby actually made her jump.

"Hello?"

Julie walked to the lobby to find one of the guys from the mail department who ran errands holding a bag of food. "Ms. Harrison?"

"Ah yes."

"Got food for you and a note that I put inside the bag." He set it down on the desk and Julie could see it came from the Mexican restaurant she and Luke had been headed for when she'd left. "Paid in advance including the tip." He waved and backed away. "Gotta run. More stops." He took off for the hallways.

Julie's stomach and her nose applauded the wonderful smells coming from the bag and she quickly went to find the note.

> I planned to eat this with you, but Blake called and has something he wants me to see regarding that situation we discussed. I'm not calling because I'm going to pick you up from work and if I call you can tell me not to.
>
> Luke
>
> PS Lock the lobby door.

Julie leaned on the desk. Luke hadn't let her walk away.

Chapter Thirteen

Leaving Julie when there was so much tension between them was killing Luke, but keeping her safe had to come first. Twenty minutes after sending her the lunch order and note, Luke sat behind his desk on his computer at Walker Security, waiting for Blake to arrive and trying to figure out how Elizabeth Moore's sister had gotten his phone number. And there it was. A proposal Royce had submitted for several charity events involving Elizabeth Moore that included Luke's phone number. That was how the sister had gotten his number. She must have Elizabeth's computer or charity documents. Nothing overtly sinister and he hoped like hell that was the case all together. After reading the journal, he wasn't so sure.

Blake walked through the front door from the street, with two men on his heels, both stiff, in slacks and button downs, with faces made from stone. Cops or some type of law enforcement, Luke decided instantly. He didn't get up. It wasn't that he didn't respect those who protected the innocent. He'd simply been around the track enough times to know everyone who was supposed to be a good guy wasn't, and many who were still pulled the power play every chance they could find.

"This is Brian Murphy," Blake said, indicating the stocky black man who stood at his right shoulder. "He's ATF and he saved my ass a time or two."

Murphy won Luke's immediate attention and his respect. Luke dropped his feet to the floor and stood.

Murphy, who looked at least ten years older than Blake, laughed low and hearty as he extended his hand to Luke across the desk. "Yeah, the kid was wild, but he kept things interesting. We miss him."

Luke rounded the desk, accepting Murphy's hand. "He's still wild, trust me. He doesn't seem to understand that red sports cars, motorcycles, and women by the bucket come with some downsides, like danger."

Murphy chuckled and ran his fingers over his chin. "I think that might be exactly what he likes about those things." He indicated the tall man standing next to him with sandy brown hair and closely set untrusting eyes. "This guy here is Tom Hendrix."

"DEA," Blake said, "and I haven't worked with him but he's on a task force with Brian that you'll find interesting."

Luke gave the man a quick once over and a nod, crossing his arms without an offer of his hand. Hendrix wasn't eager to offer his hand either. Luke didn't like him, but that didn't mean the man wasn't good at his job.

"Ex-SEAL, I hear?" Hendrix asked.

"That's right," Luke said, and then motioned to a few chairs. "Why don't we sit and you can fill me in on this task force."

"Don't mind if I do," Blake said, claiming a chair. Murphy sat down next to him. Hendrix leaned on the desk across from Luke. Luke stayed as he was, arms still crossed, legs in a V.

Blake pressed the conversation onward. "I used some connections to check out the names in the journal you were given. Dragonfly pulled up nothing, but Paul Arel gave me a hard agency hit."

Luke arched a brow. "I'm listening."

"He's a French-Canadian Citizen who owns a jewelry store he uses as his excuse for travel," Murphy said. "He's also the leader of a cartel that is a little too good at the money laundering used to hide their drug and weapons operations. We haven't been able to nail them."

"We need to have enough hard evidence to take him down and keep him down," Hendrix said. "And it sounds like this Ms. Harrison has a way in through the doors we need open."

Luke didn't like the sound of this. "How exactly is that? She's got a journal with names. Nothing more."

"Arel is a big art fanatic," Hendrix said. "Not only is he suspected of having some highly-sought after stolen pieces in his personal collection, but he buys expensive, even rare art, with illegal money, and then transports it across international lines."

"Then resells it here on this side of the border for the cash," Blake added. "The illegal money becomes perfectly legal."

"And the connection Julie has is Judge Moore," Luke said, thinking there was no way he was letting Julie snoop around for these guys.

"That's right," Hendrix said. "And as of this morning, Ms. Harrison agreed to take over a charity event that Judge Moore's wife was supposed to host tomorrow night."

Luke didn't let his surprise show, but damn it, he'd told her to stay away from Moore. "And you know this how?"

"We have the judge well monitored," Hendrix said.

As in wire taps, Luke assumed. "She's not playing bait or even snitch, so don't ask."

"Look, Luke," Murphy said. "I know this woman matters to you. But if she is on Arel's radar, which I suspect she is, then she isn't safe until he goes down."

"If she's on his radar," Luke said. "She won't be an easy source of information. And surely you have agents inserted close to her."

"We do. Well, we did." Tom ran his hand across his jaw. "We have an agent missing."

Silence filled the room. After a long moment, Luke said, "How close are you to getting someone new inside?"

"They aren't," Blake said. "That's why they want Julie to help."

"And a new agent will need time to build trust," Murphy added, "that we don't have."

"There's more at stake here than you know," Blake said, "or I wouldn't even have brought them here. They've linked tainted drugs to these guys. The stories in the news about the rising cases of teen overdoses the past few months? They aren't overdoses. The drugs they're taking are tainted. Arel has to go down."

Luke walked to the window and stared out at the street without really seeing it. He didn't want Julie in this and he only knew one way around that. He turned back to the men. "I'll get inside the operation."

"How the hell are you going to do that?" Blake asked.

"I'll attend the art show and convince the judge that I have a secret hobby to support a few expensive habits."

"And that would be what?" Hendrix asked.

"I acquire art that no one else can get their hands on...for a price."

A slow smile slid onto his brother's lips and Blake leaned back and slid his hands behind his head. "Pretty smart, for a SEAL."

He'd convinced his brother he had a good plan. Now, he just had to convince Julie that not only was this a good plan, but that he was a good plan for her. Every second he was with her, he was more certain. The problem was, the more certain he became about her, the less she seemed to be about him. It would bother him if he let himself think about it, and even mess with his head. He'd never put himself on the line like this with a woman as he was with Julie. But he couldn't let it mess with his head, any more than he could let her push him away, because she needed him, even if she didn't know it. She was deep into something dirty and dangerous that could easily turn deadly.

***

It was nearly nine at night by the time Julie stepped onto the elevator after a partner meeting to head back to her floor. She texted Luke as she'd promised and let him know she was almost ready to leave, despite a long list of things to do. The worst thing on that list was the absolute need to take off the next afternoon to handle the charity event. She loved doing charity work, especially for kids, but the timing and the complete lack of preparation the judge's email had indicated made this one a small crisis at a bad time.

She exited the elevator and walked past Gina's long-abandoned desk, drawing up short at the sight of Luke waiting on her in her office.

"You trying to starve me or what?" he asked, shutting his laptop he had open on top of her conference table.

She would never get used to how her skin heated just from seeing this man. "How long have you been waiting?"

He indicated the wrappers on the desk. "Long enough to eat two Snickers and a bag of crackers and be hungry all over again."

"I'm sorry," she said. "I thought you were going to wait until I texted you. I'll grab my purse and we can eat. I'm starving, too." When she would have walked to her desk, he pulled her into his arms.

"I'm starving, too," he said. "For you. Did you miss me?"

His voice was low, his breath a warm, teasing trickle against her lips and from anyone else, at any other time in her life, that question would have led her to a fun, flirtatious retort. With Luke, it was filled with implication, and still she found herself saying, "Yes. Yes, I did."

The air in the room thickened instantly and crackled with a spark that could easily turn to outright fire. "Good," he said, his thumb stroking her cheek. "Because after you left me out there on the sidewalk I wasn't so sure."

"You're very good at making me do crazy things I shouldn't do."

He smiled. "So it was my fault?"

"Of course," she teased. "Everything is the man's fault, unless he's my client or you feed me. Seriously. I'm starving." She kissed him and pushed out of his arms. "I'm getting my purse."

Twenty minutes later, they'd walked a few blocks down the road to one of New York's many wonderful hole-in-the-wall pizza joints, many of which Julie frequented probably too often.

"We have the place to ourselves," she said, settling at one of the tiny white tables with her giant slice of cheese pizza.

Luke joined her with two equally giant slices of pepperoni. "So," he said, watching her fold her pizza like a sandwich and take a big bite. "Tell me about the charity event tomorrow night."

She almost choked, and grabbed her drink to swallow. "How could you possibly know that?" she asked, when she finally recovered.

He leaned in closer. "The judge's phones were tapped even before we planned the same."

"So the police suspect he killed her?"

"It's even bigger than that," he said, and she listened as he recounted what he'd learned that day.

Cartel. She was involved with a cartel. Julie sat back. "I'm suddenly not hungry. I don't know how I got in the middle of this. I've always tried to stay out of the way of trouble."

"More importantly is how we get you out of it," he said. "And the best way to do that is to get me inside this thing and back you out."

"How?"

"I'll go as your date," he said. "You introduce me and I'll pull him aside, make it clear you don't know what he has going on or what I have going on. Then, I'll make sure he, and his connections, know I can get those elusive pieces of art their hearts desire, for a price."

She felt outright sick now. "You're going to put yourself in the center of a cartel to get me out of it." She'd been around the Walker brothers enough to know how they operated. They were protectors. So much so that she wondered if that wasn't what was really drawing Luke to her now. Maybe this was sex, and some manly duty. He'd already given her the 'we'll stay friends no matter what' lecture. And with any other man, she would have said, 'perfect'. A sexy affair and no strings, no emotional bonds. And no chance of getting hurt. She swallowed hard.

"Julie," Luke said, drawing her gaze from where it had settled on her slice of pizza.

She nodded. "Yes?"

"I'm getting you out of this, yes, and I won't pretend that isn't a huge motivator to me. I won't let anything happen to you."

"I know," she said, her throat threatening to close. God, who was she? Nothing used to rattle her. Nothing but...Luke.

His eyes narrowed. "What does that mean?"

"It means I'm glad you're involved," she said, and she meant that. He might break her heart in the end, but she'd be alive to feel the pain. That beat dead any day of the week. "You said cartel. Are we talking drugs? Weapons?"

"Yes to both, but the part of this equation that makes this bigger than usual is that not only are they selling illegal drugs, and targeting teens."

"I've seen a few news pieces on teens dying," she said. "This cartel is responsible?"

"The drugs are tainted."

Julie drew in a breath that rasped through her lungs like acid. Kids were her soft spot. They always had been. Kids who wanted to believe in the adults around them, and often did so with trust that wasn't deserved. "Then consider me in for the count. Whatever I have to do, I'll do it without hesitation."

"You just have to get me to the judge and play the role of my unsuspecting, trusting love." He glanced at her pizza. "And eat." The strong line of his always sexy mouth curved, "You'll need your strength to practice that role later."

At that moment, getting lost in Luke sounded pretty darn good, and maybe she'd even let herself play the role of the blind, smitten lover. Playing the role, whatever it might be, had gotten her through a lot in life. In fact, maybe she simply needed to stop thinking so much with Luke.

"A few games with you might be just what I need," she said, leaning forward and picking up her pizza, and glancing at his. "But I suggest you eat, too. I'm not going to be easy on you."

They finished up their pizza, and stepped into the chilly night air, walking back toward her building where Luke had parted, and a chill slid down Julie's spine that had nothing to do with the temperature. Suddenly, she was more than a little aware of how that area of town, while highly populated during the day, was almost empty at night. So much for not thinking too much.

Luke seemed to sense her unease, pulling her under his strong arm, his big body warming her. "Nice to walk these streets when you aren't getting pushed and shoved, now isn't it?"

She slid her arm under his leather jacket, craving the feel of his hard body, his strength, next to hers. "Tonight, I think a crowd and some pushing and shoving might feel good."

"Crowds give a false sense of security," he said. "You never know what's hiding in a crowd."

"If you were a doctor you'd have a horrible bedside manner."

He smiled down at her. "I did pretty good with your cut," he reminded her, and boy did he. She barely remembered it an hour later. "How's it doing?"

She lifted her band-aid. "Other than the really lousy style statement, better."

"Maybe we should stick to takeout," he said. "No cleanup." He motioned to a side street by her building. "The garage was full. I had to snag a meter."

"There are a lot of medical offices in the building and it gets busy on Mondays," she said. "I should have told you to park in my spot that I never use." The hair on the nape of her neck stood up, and she could feel the slight, barely there stiffening of Luke's spine beneath her palm.

"I never mind a walk," he said, but his tone had changed, tightened. He lifted a hand to indicate the truck. "There we are."

He clicked the locks open as they approached, and she was aware of the full paid-parking area they were passing, that sense of something being under the bed, or in this case, the cars, making her want to run. And her imagination was exactly why she didn't watch scary movies.

Luke opened the door for her and helped her inside, his voice low as he handed her his phone. "Blake's on speed dial. Tell him we have an unwelcome visitor and keep him on the line." He started to hand her the keys. "Don't turn anything on. In fact, don't touch anything. Just call Blake after you lock the doors." He shut the door.

Chapter Fourteen

L uke wanted to get Julie the hell out of here, but he had to deal with the very real possibility his vehicle could have been tampered with. They had company, and it wasn't the kind that came around on holidays, irritated you, and left. Luke sauntered away from her door, his posture deceptively relaxed, a whistle on his lips. The paid parking lot to Luke's right, filled with at least thirty vehicles, was like that crowd he'd said was dangerous. There were lots of places to hide, but the guy under the Jeep several feet back wasn't as good as he thought he was.

Luke walked around the back of the truck, out of Julie's sight, his skin twitching, his nerve endings were so on edge. He pretended to walk toward the driver's door, shrugging out of his coat as if he meant to throw it on the seat, when he actually wanted the ease of movement getting rid of it gave him.

He dropped down to the ground, removed the gun under his pant leg, and let the coat lie on the ground, already moving forward. Luke was in the parking lot, using the vehicles for cover before the man could have processed what was happening.

He found cover by a sweet little ride, a Mustang Shelby, using the wheel to hide his feet and squatting under the vehicle to look for the would-be attacker, now turned into Luke's prey.

He listened and watched. There was a scrape and then a shadow. Luke lunged forward as the guy darted between vehicles, grabbed the man by the shirt, fully intending to slam him against a car and find out who'd sent him and who his target was tonight. Was it him or Julie or both?

"Release him," came a low, accented order.

Luke rose to his feet and pulled his capture to his chest, and pressing the gun to the man's temple. The other man shot Luke's human shield right between his eyes. The shooter took off running.

Shit shit shit. Luke's heart lodged in his throat at the fear he'd done exactly what had been planned, and left Julie alone in the truck. He tossed aside the dead guy, and with his finger on the trigger, guarding his back, he ran for the truck, scared like he'd never been scared in his life.

The instant he rounded the cars and saw Julie looking desperately through the window, he exhaled the air lodged in his throat with his heart.

She opened the door and he blocked her exit. "Oh God, what-?"

He held up a silencing finger and her eyes went to his gun and then widened. She nodded. He took the phone, knowing his brother would be one the line. "One down and another armed and missing and I'm not risking the truck being hot, not to mention we're also sitting ducks. I'm headed south and into the subway." He hung up, knowing his brother would get the right people here, his hand sliding to Julie's hair. "Stay close and do exactly what I say."

"We could run for the building."

He shook his head. "That's where they expect us to run. The subway is two blocks. We're safer there. Take off your shoes and carry them. They'll slow you down and make noise." She nodded and stuffed them in her purse before sliding it over her shoulder cross-ways. She gave him a nod of readiness, brave when most would not have been.

He lifted her out of the truck and squatted, hoping they looked like they were just blocked by the door. "We'll be fine." He didn't wait for her reply. He tugged her around the door, and took off running with her pulled close to his side. The next three minutes were eternal. When they finally hit the subway stairs, he stuffed his gun in his pants and Julie slipped on her shoes. They kept running and he lifted her over the entrance machines, not about to take time to buy a ticket. They ignored the screams of other riders and kept going.

Luke herded them onto a train a second before the doors shut, uncaring of where it was going. With Julie's hand in his he walked to the far end of the car, away from the other ten or so riders, and grabbed a pole to hold on to.

Julie wrapped her arms around him, and staring down at her, all he could think was how easily she could have died tonight. He lowered his mouth and kissed her, needing her right then as he had never needed her in his life.

When he finally got her back to his place, he'd already talked to Blake, and knew he and the task force, were already at the truck and dealing with fallout and investigation.

Luke led Julie to the couch and sat her down, going down on one knee. "You okay?"

"Now, that we're here, yes. Luke, what was that back there?"

"I don't know yet," he said. Something about the entire thing was off. Why shoot your own man? That just didn't add up. "Right now, why don't you put my massive tub to use? It hasn't even been properly broken in. I'm sure Lauren has about anything you might need and I can promise you we're locked down like Fort Knox here. You're safe. Go try and relax and I'll try and get us answers.

She hesitated. "My feet are disgusting," she said. "I'll have to shower before I can even take a bath."

He smiled. "Your feet? After all you just went through that's what's on your mind?" That's what's upsetting you?"

"Now that I'm here and alive, yes. Do have any idea how disgusting those streets are?"

She was tough, tougher than she gave herself credit for. And he was afraid she might need to be a whole lot tougher before this was over.

***

Luke sat on a barstool at Blake's island kitchen bar, watching his brother pace as he talked on the phone. He ended the call and set his phone on the counter.

"No body found," he said. "No blood. No signs of struggle."

Luke gave a slow nod. "So whoever didn't want the guy to talk didn't want him identified either."

"Yeah," Blake said. "No doubt the dude's going to end up at the bottom of a river somewhere with concrete blocks on his feet. I imagine that was what would have happened to the two of you. You'd have gone missing. Forever."

"No body, no murder," Luke said. "Am I the only one that thinks Moore wouldn't risk the connection of his soon-to-be ex's death, and that of his divorce attorney?"

"I'm right there with you, thinking the same thing," Blake said, sauntering to the fridge to pull out a jug of chocolate milk. He downed a gulp before bringing it with him to sit across from Luke. "So either you were the target, which still is awfully closely linked to Julie, or-"

"Judge Moore wasn't behind this."

"Arel might try to kill off Julie if he thinks she knows something she shouldn't," Blake suggested. "It makes sense he'd kill off Elizabeth and Julie."

"Would he want Judge Moore under investigation if Moore is instrumental in the art used for the money laundering? And I keep going back to shooting your own guy and then getting rid of the body. That's big."

"Where are you going with this?"

"I don't know but we have a judge involved. We could have law enforcement involved. Someone doesn't like me and/or Julie in this thing. And who knows just how involved we are?"

"I asked Murphy and Hendrix to keep things on the down low, so maybe five people on the task force make that list, and then Elizabeth's sister, and anyone else she or Julie told that Julie has the journal."

"Julie's too smart to run her mouth," Luke said. "We should get Diana into a safe house somewhere in case someone decides she has it or she knows too much."

"We don't know she's innocent herself," Blake said.

"But this way we have her under our watch anyway."

"Good point. I'll put someone on it, and I'll have them pick her brain for anything we can use to protect you and Julie. And you need to consider locking Julie down, too, man. She's too close to this. Don't fuck up like I did with my woman and lose her."

Right. Lock Julie down. Piece of cake. Luke had a feeling he was about to see a war unlike any he'd ever known.

***

Gina stood in front of her full-length mirror and smiled. Dressed in a white lace bra and panty set with matching garter and hose, she looked like the perfect angel she wanted her stranger to believe her to be . At least, when she opened her door.

Soft waves of silky auburn brown hair fell over her shoulders, pink lipstick defined a seductive pout, and she was already getting wet just thinking about showing her sexy French man how bad a good girl could be.

She didn't make dinner. They could order out when they came up for air. A wicked smile played on her lips.

If they came up for air.

The jangle of the telephone forced her to put her thoughts on hold. With an irritated huff she picked up the receiver from her nightstand.

"Hello," she said abruptly.

"Such hostility, Gina, dear, and to think I once thought you were sweet."

Gina frowned and sat on the edge of the bed. "Who is this?"

"You can call me Judge or Master, or whatever you prefer, since we'll soon be very close friends."

The voice suddenly rang a bell. "Judge Moore. How did you get this number?"

"That's not what's important," he said. "What's important is what a blast in the past you were, my dear. Silk sheets and naughty toys do it for you, right honey? Or is it backseats, and dingy motels? H....Yes. That's it, isn't it? You never made it to high society call girl."

Gina's hand trembled. "What do you want?"

"Come to the El Toronto hotel tomorrow at noon. I'll show you my cards, if you, shall we say, show me yours. Room 311 will give you a trip to paradise, sugar."

The line went dead.

Gina grabbed the phone and flung it across the room, tearing it with a force that tore the plug from the wall. This was crap! She had covered her tracks! No way could this be happening.

She paced, she muttered, she cursed. Finally, she calmed. She sat back down on the bed. Somehow, someway, she would turn this around in her favor. Judge Moore was going to regret messing with her. If he thought sex was intimidation, he could go to hell. Sex to her was entertainment, plain and simple.

The doorbell rang as if on cue. Sex with a sexy Frenchman. She needed it. She deserved it. Tomorrow Judge Moore would learn not to cross her. Tonight her Frenchman would get a taste of paradise of his own.

She drew a breath and calmed herself. A slow smile slid to her lips and she made her way to the door, her pink high-heeled shoes clicking on the floor as she moved. She wore nothing but her lingerie and saw no reason to bother with more.

Opening the door she took in Marco's jeans, a t-shirt, and a leather jacket, his chin-length brown hair a bit wild, like she hoped the man would be. His gaze raked hungrily over her body, lingering at her breasts, and then on the barely there lace between her legs. "Well now, cherie, you certainly know how to greet a man."

She curled her finger at him. "You ain't seen nothing yet, sweetheart."

Marco sauntered forward, his eyes dark, the set of his mouth arrogant. He stopped beside her, again looking her up and down with penetrating eyes, lazy and slow, in his perusal.

"Shut the door, cherie," he ordered in a soft, authoritative voice that was both deep and seductive. "What is between us is not for de neighbors eyes." He ran his finger slowly down the middle of her cleavage. " Tres belle," he said before stepping forward, and leaving her at the door.

Gina shut the door and turned to watch him as he casually inspected her living room. There was an air of danger to Marco that turned her on, made her hot and wet and wanting. He was sex personified with a truly stellar ass, and thighs like steel.

She wet her lips in anticipation, but didn't pursue, not until she got a read on him. He turned to face her, leaning lazily against her fireplace, one elbow on the mantel. The look on his face told her he wanted her to come to him. She knew the look. He wanted the power, the ultimate control. She'd played the submissive role too many times to count. For this man, she would happily play it again.

She tilted her head, studying him, wondering how he brought out the searing desire to please in her. Never before had she reacted quite so completely to a man.

Dangerous.

The word danced in her head, provoking her desire and her fears, all at once.

She took pleasure in the heat of his smoldering gaze as he watched her approach. Stopping in front of him, she let her robe drop to the floor.

His eyes were the blue of a perfect summer sky. He shrugged out of his jacket and flung it on the couch before sitting down. He stared up at her. "Strip for me, cherie."

She wanted more foreplay, to feel this man's sexy hands on her body. "And if I don't?"

He stood up, stepping forward in a fluid motion, his stance predatory, his eyes glinting with intent. "Then I will have to do it for you."

Before Gina knew what he was going to do, he had wrapped one arm around her waist while using his free hand to rip off her panties. She gasped as his hand sunk between her legs.

"Already wet," he said making a disapproving sound. "You make my job so easy, cherie. I thought you would be more of a challenge."

She laughed in disbelief. "Say that after you make me come."

A slow smile lifted the corners of his mouth. "Have no doubt. Come, and come again, you will, and then you will beg for more." He tangled his hand into her hair and dragged her mouth to his. "I will make you feel so good you might think you have died and gone to heaven, cherie."

Chapter Fifteen

Luke discovered Julie sitting in the dim glow of a lamp in front of the gas fireplace in his living room, wearing one of his t-shirts, with a big blanket he kept in a closet under her, and another over her legs. He found himself unable to move for the impact the sight had on him. A sense of rightness filled him. She belonged here with him, and he could easily get used to seeing her here and having her in his life.

She seemed to sense him watching her and twisted around. "Hey," she said softly, and he could hear the concern in her voice, the uncertainty.

"Hey," he replied, holding up her briefcase. "Got your things from the truck." He set it on the hall table and walked toward her, forcing himself to go slow when he'd never wanted to rush so much in his life. He had to get a grip, to pull back, to give her a chance to let down those damnable walls he wanted to tear down.

"That's great," she said. "So the truck hadn't been tampered with?"

"No. It was fine." Luke sat down next to her. "How are you?"

She wet her pale lips, her face scrubbed free of make up, her hair soft and shiny and freshly washed. She'd never looked so beautiful. "It wasn't a random mugging or car jacking attempt back there, was it?" she asked, bypassing his question.

"No," he said simply, tucking hair behind her ear. "It wasn't."

"You said there was a body, when you called Blake from the truck."

"I grabbed our intended attacker and his partner shot him."

Distress furrowed her brow. "Who was he?"

"The body disappeared."

She stiffened. "Disappeared. Oh my God, Luke. This is...terrifying. Who did this? Who sent them? Judge Moore? This cartel leader?"

"I don't think it was Moore," he said. "The man has too much to lose by the attention his wife and his divorce attorney dying would lend. And frankly, I can't see the cartel doing it either. It brings attention to the judge."

"Maybe they think he's a problem and want him out of the picture."

"Then they kill him," he said. "That shuts him up. Getting him arrested makes him talk."

"So then who?"

"I don't know," he said. "Someone who thinks we know something we shouldn't or thinks we're close to finding it out. Maybe the person Elizabeth called Dragonfly. Maybe someone we don't even know about." He pulled the cover away from her and eased her to her back, trapping one of her legs with his. "I've never been as scared as when I realized I'd left you exposed in the truck with a shooter on the loose. I could hardly breathe for fear I'd just made the worst mistake of my life."

She laughed but without humor. "You Walker men do the protect and serve thing well. I'm fine."

"Protect and serve?" he asked, pulling back to look at her. "Like you're my duty?"

"Everyone is your duty. That's what you brothers do. You protect everyone. It's what comes natural."

"You're not my duty, Julie," he said, amazed at how easily she dismissed what was between them. "Or I wouldn't have felt like I was dying inside just thinking I might have lost you."

Her lashes lowered, dark half circles on the pale perfection of her skin. "Luke."

He caressed her cheek. "Look at me."

"I can't," she said, her bottom lip trembling.

"Look at me," he ordered, his voice still soft, but with a demand this time, and slowly she obeyed, letting him see the uncertainty only he seemed to create in her. "You think this is nothing, this thing going on between us, don't you?"

"I don't know what you mean."

"Yes," he insisted, teasing her lips with his, "you do. You know exactly what I mean. It's not nothing and if that's what want it to be, I should warn you right now. You matter to me, Julie, like I've never let any woman matter to me." He claimed her mouth with his, unable and unwilling to hear her reply. No woman had ever had this power over him, this ability to hurt him, and he'd just given her more. He didn't want her objections or her rejection. He wanted her acceptance, her passion, and some part of him knew she wasn't ready to give it to him, not with words.

Luke parted her lips, pressing his tongue past her teeth, tasting her with a slow caress.

She moaned into his mouth, and the deliciously erotic sound had his cock expanding against his zipper, making him wish he'd done away with their clothes. Her fingers laced into his hair, giving him a tiny piece of her submission, so tiny, so far from all he wanted. She didn't submit during sex, not even with him. Not in the past, but she had several nights before, and he wanted it again. He wanted that invisible sign of trust, of feeling something for him that she might not put into words, but showed him instead. With her body, her response to his touch, his kiss, his body buried deep inside hers.

His hand slid down her back, under the shirt and around her ass before he caressed the slender dip of her waist, and cupped her naked breasts.

She whimpered as he teased her nipple, her hips arching into his hand. He trailed his mouth down her jaw, over her neck, to her ear.

"I love those little sounds you make." He shoved her shirt upward and she helped him pull it over her head, but Luke didn't let her. He wrapped it around her hands and held them there, running his hand over her breasts, tweaking her nipple.

"I can do a lot more with my hands free, you know?"

"You can have them back after you come for me," he said, his palm traveling down her stomach, his leg pulling hers open.

"That's a—"

She gasped as he caressed and teased the silky heat between her legs. "There we go," he said. "That's exactly what I was looking for."

He licked her nipple and she arched her back, thrusting her voluptuous breasts higher. Luke sucked one stiff peak into his mouth, and sunk two fingers inside her.

"Ah," she panted. "I...Oh. I want to touch you."

"Not until you give me what I asked for," he said, his lips moving to hers, his tongue tracing the seam of her mouth, his fingers stroking her inner walls in a slow back and forth motion, even as his thumb played with her swollen nub. "Not until you give me what I want."

"Just so you know," she whispered. "I'm going to pay you back for this."

He smiled. "I hope you do."

"Oh I will," she said, "and..."

He let go of her hands and slid between her legs to suckle her clit. She tensed instantly and began spasming around his fingers. He suckled and licked and brought her to a complete release. The instant he felt her relax, she tugged at his shirt, and he fully intended to let her pull it off of him. Only she didn't. She knotted it at his hands.

He laughed and sat up on his knees, arching a brow. She was on her knees too, making sure the shirt was tightly nodded. "Sit back against the couch."

"You do know I still have my pants and my boots on? It would be easier to take them off with my hands free."

"I can handle it," she said, shoving his chest. "Sit back."

Who was he to argue with the hottest woman in the planet? He sat back against the couch, between the coffee table and the love seat. She shoved the coffee table away, those lush breasts bouncing with the movement, and he was pretty sure he was about as hard as he'd ever been his entire life.

She tugged at his boot. Again, her breasts bounced. He groaned. "You know you're driving me crazy, don't you?"

"You earned it," she reminded him.

Yes, he supposed he did, but with Julie, she always gave as good as she got. He reminded himself it was one of the things that made her so damn hot. Nothing was easy with her, but it was always fucking phenomenal.

The instant his boots were gone she settled between his legs and caressed her way up his thighs. "Did I mention that your sounds of pleasure make me hot?" she asked.

"Then I'm pretty damn sure you're about to make us both hot."

A teasing smiled played on her gorgeous mouth. It had given him more than a few fantasies over the years and it was a mouth he knew could do some pretty amazing things. She bent over and pressed her breasts to his crotch, taking his bound hands in hers and sliding her lush curves up his stomach and chest until she urged his hands behind his head. Her breasts were now in his face and he captured one with his mouth, suckling it deeply, roughly.

Julie moaned and held onto his head, rolling her shoulders forward in pleasure before pushing him back from her. "Stop," she ordered, her blue eyes finding his. The connection was jarring in its intensity, the emotion between them far deeper than the erotic play of this game.

For an instant, he saw that vulnerable side of her flash in her eyes before the sexy, sinful, confident woman claimed his mouth in a sizzling kiss, and then drug her lips down his neck. She kissed her way downward and the snap of his pants, the slide of his zipper, seemed to magnify and echo through the room.

The instant her hand was inside his pants, adrenaline sent a rush to his head. Her fingers stroked the soft skin of his shaft, and then pulled the hard length of him free. She leaned and licked the pooled liquid at the tip and then suckled just the head of him into her mouth before tugging at his waistband.

"You can keep the socks, but nothing else."

Damn, how he wanted to rip his hands free, and he could, but the desire to enjoy the woman in control gave him his own control, his own will to resist. By the time they'd worked together to free him of his clothes, he was thick and pulsing and all but going insane with the need for release.

She bent over, sticking that gorgeous ass of hers in the air, wrapping her hand around the base of his cock. She looked at him, scraping her teeth over her lip.

"Now what should I do?"

"Witch."

"Tell me. Your wish is my command."

"All right then," he said. "Suck me."

She smiled. "All right then, I will." She bent down and cut him a taunting look. "After I lick you." She rolled her tongue around him and Luke moaned. She licked him up and down, and watching her was almost as good as what she was doing to him. She was driving him crazy.

"Suck me," he groaned. "You—" She took him into her mouth. Oh and how she took him. The woman knew how to please him, and she'd practiced plenty during that summer month they'd spent together. She sucked, and pumped, and used her hand, her lips, her tongue, until he couldn't even hold his eyes open, the pleasure was so intense. He leaned back, his head on the cushion, and when he would have said 'harder' and 'faster' she was already there, and so was he. Release came over him, intense and ripping through him with biting, painfully good pleasure. Slowly, he relaxed, the tension in his muscles easing. Julie climbed on top of him and he tore his hands free, wrapping his arms around her and kissing her.

"You know you drive me wild," he said, "but not because of this. Because of you and us, and-"

She pressed her lips to his, silencing his words, and he was certain it was because she didn't want his confession, because he'd let her slip back into the sex goddess routine too quickly. But then she surprised him, and murmured, "I know."

He pulled back, forced her to look at him. "You know what?"

Her lashes lowered, then lifted. "That it's more than...me driving you wild or you driving me wild. I know."

They stared at each for several intense seconds before they were kissing again, wild and hot, a craving that had to be fulfilled. And when it shouldn't have been possible, he was hard again, thick with need.

"Let's go to the bedroom," he said, before he forgot that they needed a condom.

She reached behind her, stroking his shaft. "I like it right here." She started to lift herself and he stopped her.

"Condom."

"I'm on the pill."

He went still at that, at the idea that she hadn't been before but she was now, at the implications there had been someone else in her life.

Her fingers curled at his cheek. "I've always been," she said. "I've just never told anyone...until now."

What he'd thought was a sign that he meant nothing to her only moments before, now seemed like a gift. "I don't think I've ever wanted to be inside you as much as I do right now." He kissed her, and wrapped his arm around her, lifting her. She pressed him to the slickness of her core, before slowly inching her way down. When finally she settled fully on top of him, him buried inside her, they lingered, their mouths a breath apart, the energy in the room crackling with electricity and tension.

He pressed her down, thrusting into her, and a slow, sensual dance began. It built into something fierce, something that made them one, neither of them in control. Passion built until they were frantically touching, kissing, moving, and when they reached the edge of pleasure, she went first, and he followed.

They collapsed into each other, and clung together. No words were necessary.

***

A long time later, Luke lay with Julie on their backs in front of the fire, pressed together.

"You said you were on the pill as an extra precaution," he said, the subject weighing on his mind. For the first time in his life, he was thinking of what settling down, what a wife and kids might be like.

"Yes," she said after a long pause.

"Because you don't want kids?"

"I...no." She rolled to her side, away from him to face the fire. "I don't."

He turned to her, hugging her. "Because you had a bad childhood." It was the only thing that made sense. She volunteered for children's events, she worried about the children of divorces.

"Too often parents let their kids down."

"You aren't your mother."

"No," she said. "But there are plenty of kids I can help who have parents like mine, or kids like the ones tomorrow night is about, who need me and people like me."

Damn. Tomorrow night. This was not the best time to talk about this, but he wasn't sure there was a better one either. "Let's talk about tomorrow," he said, sitting up and pulling her up with him.

"What about tomorrow?"

His gaze slid over her breasts and he felt the stir of his body. Luke grabbed the shirt she'd tossed aside. "I can't complete many coherent sentences when you're this naked and this gorgeous."

She didn't respond and he could see the concern in her face. She tugged the shirt over her head before repeating, "What about tomorrow?"

Luke grabbed his pants, bypassing the boxers he couldn't locate to pull them on before he sat down on the couch. "We have to assume that tonight was a hit on one or both of us, and that they will come for us again."

"So you want me to do what? Go into hiding?"

"Yes," he said, in no uncertain terms. "I want to keep you here or take you underground somewhere."

"You need me to get to Judge Moore and the cartel. And I need my job."

"Surely, you have enough success to be allowed to work off-site for a while."

"I could and I'm willing to do that as long as I have a means to an end. I'm not foolish enough not to see the danger I'm in. But I can't do it indefinitely, Luke. When I say I need a real means to an end, I mean it. I have only me to count on."

That punched him in the gut and then right in the heart. "You have me and I thought we just moved somewhere towards you knowing that."

"I...We did. We did. But Luke, I have bills to think about."

"I'll help you if I need to."

"No. I'm not taking your money. To get to that point would mean the career I have worked night and day was lost. If you think that's where I'm letting this go, I'm not. I can't. And the children's charity is counting on me. I'll lay low. I'll skip work, but I won't skip that."

"Julie—"

"This is bigger than me or you," she said, going to her knees. "Stop playing my protector and think about this rationally. I'm scared. I'm scared to death, but people, children, are dying from tainted drugs this bastard is selling them."

"I'll find another way to stop him."

"We both know that the task force you talked about would have found a way in if they could. I can get you inside the operation, or I hope you're right and I can."

"No," he said, pushing to his feet.

"No?" she demanded.

"That's right. No."

She stood up. "I'm going to get dressed and leave."

He shot to his feet. "So now you're going to be irrational and go home and get killed?"

"No," she said. "I'm going to go to Royce and Lauren's apartment where I'll be safe and you can think."

"I don't need to think."

"Yes," she insisted, "you do. You need to think about waking up and reading about another dead child and knowing you could have saved that child's life by taking down this cartel." She stormed off and Luke stood there, tension curled in stomach, prickling every nerve ending he owned.

Damn it, he loved Julie. He loved her in this moment more than he'd ever loved her. She was gorgeous, and sexy, and successful because she was smart and she worked hard. But even more than that, she was scared and yet she was still brave, still willing to sacrifice for others.

He ran a hand over his face and tracked after her to the bedroom, where he found her setting her bag on the bed, to begin packing. "You aren't going to back off of this, are you?" he asked, leaning on the door frame.

She abandoned the bag again and turned to him. "I can't abandon this."

"Then you do exactly what I say, how I say it, and when I say it."

She walked to him and wrapped her arms around him, tilting her chin up to look at him. "I have no problem with that. Like I said, I'm not foolish, or without fear. A whole lot of fear actually."

"If you don't, I swear I will kidnap you and hold you hostage somewhere until I know you're safe."

Her expression softened. "I don't want to lose you either."

It was the closest thing to really admitting her feelings to him that she'd come, and he slid his hand behind her neck and pulled her mouth to his. "I'm not going to lose you."

"Good," she whispered before he kissed her and took her to bed, where he was going to do his best to convince her to stay until after Tuesday night, and the charity event with Judge Moore, was over.

***

At exactly noon on Tuesday, Gina walked into the lobby – if you could call it that – of the dingy El Toronto Hotel, unable to suppress the apprehension in her stomach. A long lunch spent reliving the past wasn't appealing. Not that she was ashamed of being a sexual person, but doing it for pleasure, and doing it with a bunch of disgusting men to pay her bills was a totally different picture. She'd been good at it too. She knew just how to make those bastards come back for more, even when part of her prayed they wouldn't.

Glancing around her surroundings she felt the sickening feeling of deja vu. One thing about New York, it did extreme well. The high end was glitzy, the low end absolute scum city. This was about as low as you could get.

Dingy brown walls, scraped up and scuffed floors, with two cheap, torn chairs as the only furnishings. She could smell the musty scent of sex, drugs, and filth as if it were a part of the very lining of the walls. Clearly, the judge was trying to make a point, to tell her just how low he believed she was, and how low those in the firm she now worked would as well.

She'd worked hard to get her life back on track and he wasn't taking that from her. Gina headed down a hallway, and up the stairs. As she reached the third floor, she flipped the record button on her cell phone, making sure every bit of this encounter was recorded. She fully intended to turn the power upside down.

She found the room she needed and knocked, no hesitation, no reason to wait. The door flew open and Judge Moore waved her in, still fully dressed in a dress shirt, tie and slacks, but the sly smile on his face told her he didn't intend to stay that way.

The door slammed behind her.

"Lock it," he ordered.

She did as he said, flipping the latch.

He stopped at the edge of the bed. She stopped at the edge of the hallway leading into the room. "Take your coat off," he said. "I'd hate for you to get hot."

She set her purse down, leaving the folds open to allow the recorder the best reception. Her coat followed but she tossed it on the bed, making sure not to cover her purse.

His gaze raked over the white lace blouse she'd changed into before arriving. It dipped low to reveal her ample cleavage and she'd paired with an equally seductive slim figure-hugging black skirt. The blatantly lustful look on his face let her know, that despite his almost ex-wife being barely in the ground, he intended to fuck her. She knew that already. Only one question remained: what else did he want?

"Like what you see, Judge?" she asked.

"Don't most men?"

"I didn't ask about most men. I asked about you."

She sashayed to him, letting her hips do a sultry dance, stopping in front of him, letting him know she wasn't about to wilt under this threats. "What are we doing here, Judge? Or should I say, Master?" She glanced around the room. "I would have thought you'd have chosen a nicer place."

"Isn't this the kind of place you prefer?"

"I moved up from this years ago, honey," she said. "I like my hotels plush and my men loaded. I hope you have lots of cash. I'm expensive."

He laughed. "So you don't mind if I pass your card out to your employers? There are eleven men and Julie, aren't there? I bet we could get you a promotion."

Her lips twitched as her gaze dropped to the bulge in his pants. "What is it you want besides the obvious, Judge?"

"It's simple enough," he said. "I want information on your boss and anyone she comes in contact with. Passwords to her private files, records of her calls, anything with my name on it, as a top priority."

She clicked her tongue on the roof of her mouth, seeing her chance for a turnabout. "Sounds like a big order. What will I get in return?"

He looked down at her breasts. "What we do," he said, tearing his gaze from her cleavage, "which I intend for us to do often, will be our little secret. Just as what you've done in the past will be as well." He reached out and shoved her blouse and her bra down to expose her nipples, teasing them with his fingers. And damn, if her body didn't respond, as it always did, even when she hated the bastard like she did this one.

"There is one condition," he said with a raspy voice.

She quirked a brow, trying to ignore the way his fingers were arousing her. "Which is?"

He ignored her question. "Unbutton your blouse," he ordered.

She didn't hesitate. Her fingers worked the buttons quickly. His lust was her power. She went down on her knees in front of him, her hand striking his zipper. "I'll give you what you want, all of it – pleasure and satisfaction. For fifty thousand dollars I'll even get you your dead wife's journal." It was a mistake. He had her up and shoved against the wall in two seconds flat. "What journal?"

Her heart thundered in her ears but she recovered from the initial surprise of his attack. It wasn't the first time she'd been roughed up. "I told you for fifty-"

He shoved a hand to her throat. "You have no idea what you are into, bitch. What journal?"

Gina grabbed at his hands, gasping for air. "Let go," she squeaked. "Let...go."

"You going to tell me what I want to know?"

"Yes. Yes."

He loosed his hold on her neck but didn't let go. "I heard Julie talking to someone named Diana about a dead person's journal. I did some research and figured out that's Elizabeth's sister."

"Where is it?"

"She and that Walker brother have it," she hissed.

"You're going to get it for me and you can forget the fifty-fucking thousand dollars. The only one who'll be paying anything is you if I don't get it. That price will be your life. The people I work with will bleed you dry to get what they want and then make you disappear."

***

Judge Moore sat on the edge of the lumpy mattress and dropped his head into his hands. "Shit," he mumbled letting the word echo through the empty room.

He had gotten himself into a hell of a mess. If Arel found out he had done him wrong he would be a dead man. Just hearing his wife had caused more trouble would be enough to make Arel mad enough to draw blood. If Arel ever found out he and Dragonfly had double-crossed him, they'd be digging their own graves.

He picked up the hotel phone, knowing the call wouldn't be traced because no one would ever know he had been there. The line rang three times before he heard a clipped hello.

"We have problems," he said without any greeting.

"Damn you, I told you to never call me at work."

"Unless you want Arel to know his trusted man Dragonfly did him wrong, you'd better listen."

Silence greeted him for several long moments in which he could tell the other man was walking, probably to privacy. Finally, he said, "Go on."

"My wife had a journal which she gave to her sister. I doubt it exposes us to the police, but she saw you with me several times. We need that journal so Arel can't get to it."

A series of muffled curses rumbled across the line. "So I'll do the sister and get the journal."

"She gave it to Julie Harrison and if you kill either of them, you know damn well it's going to bring attention on me."

"No bodies, not murder. Believe me, I know how to make people disappear."

"And if you bring me down, I'll take you with me."

More silence. "What do you propose we do then? Sit on our fucking hands?"

"I have someone close to Julie who's going to get me the journal. Once we know what's inside, we can decide what to do about anyone who's read it."

"When will you have it?"

"Soon."

"Get it and get it now, because if you don't make me feel as warm and fuzzy as a school girl in pink quickly, I'll deal with this my way."

The line went dead.

Chapter Sixteen

Tuesday flew by for Julie. She stood in Luke's bathroom, dressed in an emerald silk knee-length gown, applying her lipstick, and wondering where he'd gotten to. They'd spent the afternoon at the gallery readying it for tonight, and Luke had used the excuse of helping her to plant some surveillance equipment. The charity event included a live band and the dancing began at seven. Fortunately there were volunteers the door, so she didn't have to be there any longer than she had to be without Luke. Her nerves were jumping all over the place, but worrying about him was making her crazy. He and one of his men were going to break into the judge's house while he was at the event and look for the safe Elizabeth mentioned in the journal. And while she knew Luke was an ex-SEAL, she also knew exactly what she'd told him back at the airport. SEALs could die, too.

Voices carried from the other room and she grabbed her small cocktail purse from the bed and went looking for Luke. She found him and Blake both in all black, and there were two other, also very good looking, men — one with a short, military cut, the other with longish blonde hair that curled at the ends.

Good lord, she thought. Their mothers must have taken some sort of hormone to breed hot men. There was so much testosterone in the place she was afraid the apartment might go up in flames.

Luke pulled her under his arm, his big body warm and wonderful, and she clung to him. She didn't want him to die.

"I told you about the task force that's in on tonight. They'll be nearby watching, but we have our own team in place, and they are the only ones you are to trust, ever. I don't care who shows you a badge, the people in this room are the people you listen to."

"Okay," Julie said. "Do we think there's a problem with the task force?"

"We have a judge involved and the Dragonfly who has yet to be identified. We aren't taking any chances." He motioned to the dark haired man. "This is Jesse. He's going to be driving the cab that is taking you to the gallery."

"He's a former NYPD detective," Blake said, leaning against a counter, arms folded. "We couldn't trust that he wouldn't be recognized at the event so he'll stay out of sight. He'll be nearby if you need him though."

Jesse gave her a two-finger salute. "Your chauffeur awaits, madam."

Julie tried to smile but failed and Luke tightened his grip on her, as if he sensed how tense she was. She didn't want him to go tonight, and it was all she could not to turn to him and beg him not to.

Luke motioned to the other man, the blond. "And this is Kyle. He's our tech expert and if there is a safe in the house, he can get in."

"He also removed the snake from Lauren's apartment when she had that crazy man stalking her a while back," Blake mentioned, referencing the hell that Lauren had gone through that had led to her leaving the District Attorney's office.

"That would be me," Kyle said, and lifted the lid to a small steel case on the counter before flipping it around for her to see what looked like some sort of tiny chip. "This will be your mic. Blake will be on the other end until I take over for him, at which time, you'll have Luke back with you as well.

"You so much as need an escort to the bathroom you just say the word and I'll be there." Blake added.

Julie nodded. "Thank you, Blake."

"And he was serious about saying a word," Blake added. "I need 'a word'. Something you can say discreetly that lets me know you need me."

For an attorney known to think on her feet, Julie's mind was utterly blank. "I don't know."

"Apple," Blake said. "Orange. Oh what a beautiful day it is. A spoon full of sugar."

Julie actually laughed at that. "A spoonful of sugar?"

"It makes the medicine go down," he said, with a nod.

Julie shook her head and glanced at Luke. "You have a very strange brother."

"Yes," Luke said. "I know."

"We all know," Jesse agreed.

"Pride myself on it," Blake said, "and I still need that word or even a phrase that tells me you're in trouble. I'll have limited visual."

Julie thought a moment about what would be easily used in the mixed company she'd be in. "How about 'I have a headache'?"

The men all laughed. Julie's brows furrowed. "What's so funny about that?"

"Almost every woman given this question comes up with that answer," Blake supplied. "It's like all females are born with that excuse in their psyche."

"That's your discreet 'help' call," Luke said. "If you feel like the situation merits Kyle and Jesse coming with guns drawn, you say 'I think I'm getting a migraine."

Her stomach knotted. He was about to leave. "Okay."

Luke slapped the cover down on the mic and picked it up, then twined the fingers of his one free hands with hers. "Let's go get you wired."

She nodded because suddenly her throat was too tight to form words. A few minutes later they stood in the bedroom by the bed, and Luke used some sort of adhesive to stick the device on the inside of her bra.

His fingers skimmed her neck. "Don't leave the building and stay in the highly populated areas of the function until I get to you. It's killing me to leave you."

"Then don't," she said, her hand grasping his wrist. "Please don't go to the judge's house. He'll have moved anything of importance after Elizabeth's threat."

"Maybe," he said. "But we have to try, and tonight when his main collection is on display will make it easier to see what is left behind."

"Just come to the party with me, Luke, please. I have a bad feeling about all of this."

"If I didn't think my experience was critical to doing this, I'd send someone else, but I know how to get us in and out unnoticed. And Blake would die to protect you or I'd never even consider this."

"I don't care about me. I care about you. Just don't do this at all."

His expression softened. "I care about you and you said you wanted a means to an end. And as much as I want to lock you away someplace safe, I know it's not realistic. That means I have to find answers and end this. I have to a look in the judge's house and his safe."

"It's my fault you're even in this."

"It's not your fault," he said, pulling her into his arms. "And anywhere you are, I want to be, including at the party. So I'm going to go get this over with so I can join you."

***

Julie spent the first thirty minutes inside the Manhattan Museum of Art checking on every detail to make sure the event was going well. More than anything, she didn't want to think about what could be happening to Luke. That meant staying busy, which also allowed her to avoid the judge, and, for that matter, anyone who might want to kill her.

When her excuses to avoid mingling ran out, she stood at the edge of the main event space, large enough to host a wedding of at least five hundred. A band played a soft melody opposite from where Julie stood. White linen-covered tables surrounded a dance floor where only one couple had braved center stage thus far. Away from the tables, people in fancy dresses and suits stood in groups, chatting.

Julie headed for the tables, deciding to make the rounds and thank everyone for coming. She'd just finished chatting with the first table of ten when she felt a light tap on her shoulder.

"Julie."

She swung around to see Gina standing in front of her with her arm linked through that of an Adonis with dark hair and piercing eyes.

"Gina," Julie said taking in Gina's white silk dress with appreciation. Her hair was pulled up with tiny ringlets of curls around her face. "You look lovely tonight. Like an angel."

The man laughed, and Gina elbowed him. "This is Marco, my very rude date. Marco, this is Julie Harrison, my boss."

He gave a gallant half bow. "Pleased indeed, Ms. Harrison." There was a strong accent to his voice that Julie couldn't quite place.

He straightened, and Julie didn't miss the way his gaze lingered on her cleavage. He was good-looking but there was something almost predatory about him.

"Marco is an artist," Gina inserted.

"Really?" Julie said. "What kind of art?"

"My art, like my interests are broad," he said, and there was no missing the undertone of flirtation. Julie's gaze slid to Gina's face with concern, but Gina didn't seem to notice.

"I'm sure this is an interesting night for you two then," she said. "I hope you'll enjoy the event. You deserve it. Thank you for making phone calls and juggling so much to help me this morning."

"It was my pleasure," she said, "and I'll be glad to help with anything you need tonight."

Was there a condescending tone to her voice? And had it been there before and Julie hadn't noticed? Or maybe paranoia had just taken over. "It seems like all is well, so I'd say go have a good evening." Julie motioned toward a corridor to the right of the band. "The judge's collection is down that hallway and it truly is spectacular."

"All right," Gina said, "but I have my cell if anything changes."

***

Gina tightened her grip on Marco's arm as they walked away from Julie. "Why don't we take a stroll in the back courtyard?" she suggested.

"It's rather cold," he said, casting her a dark stare. "And you aren't wearing much in the way of clothes. Not that I'm complaining."

"I'm sure you'll keep me warm." There was a reason she'd invited her starving artist along for the ride. He needed money. So did she, and the judge's threats only served one purpose. He'd convinced her he'd pay far more than fifty thousand dollars. Oh, he might try to kill her, too, but Marco had a shadowy past, a way he moved and operated that told her he was more than he let on. She could feel it, almost taste it when she was with him. It turned her on. It also made her confident fate had thrown him into her path for a reason. The two of them could get rich together.

She wasn't quite ready to bring him in yet though. She had a way of getting men to open up in bed. She'd take him for a few more rides, starting in the courtyard. She'd test him, size him up. If she was right, then she'd have her man, the journal, and enough money to disappear. Screw Julie and her law degree, and screw the judge who though he could fuck her and not get fucked himself.

***

Forty-five minutes outside the city, Luke squatted in the bushes at the back Judge Moore's Long Island mansion, with Kyle by his side. It was only seven o'clock, still early for breaking and entering, but the two-acre lot and a heavy coverage of trees helped offer coverage. Impressive as always, Kyle dismantled the security system in all of about sixty seconds, including the motion detector spotlights. Luke followed Kyle silently through the back door, blending into the darkness. Working with an unspoken understanding, they split up and began their search. Luke crept along the walls, looking for a hidden panel that might be a safe or hidden compartment, keeping low to avoid the windows. A quick flash of light, two blinks as a signal, told him Kyle had found something.

Within seconds, Luke and Kyle were side-by-side in a small library just off the kitchen, where Kyle had found a basement door under a carpet.

Kneeling down, they examined the entrance where a combination lock was set inside a steel door. Kyle grinned, showing white teeth against the darkness of the room, clearly telling Luke his job would be a piece of cake.

Leaning back on his heels, Luke watched Kyle in action for all of another sixty seconds. The man was incredible. They were just about to lift he door when a tiny click made both of them freeze. They listened. There it was again, a low, barely there sound. Luke pulled the Glock at his ankle and motioned for Kyle to keep working.

Luke quickly, soundlessly, crossed the room, and flattened against the wall. Cautiously he leaned forward, surveying the hallway. When he was certain he would be undetected, he moved through the doorway.

He was halfway down the walkway when a faint creaking drew him up short. To anyone else it might have sounded like the house settling. To Luke, it sounded like they had company, and nowhere near his team's skill, or they wouldn't have been detected.

Adrenaline surged in Luke's veins and he squatted down, on the move again, pausing to glance around the wall into the living room. Two big men, also in all black, weresearching the living room, and clearly they hadn't done their surveillance well, or they'd have noticed the security system was down. They'd have known someone else was here.

Luke watched as they searched walls, behind pictures, and in unexpected spots like under the couch. Sizing up the situation, Luke backtracked. If Kyle had already found what they needed, then they could exit without the amateurs ever noticing.

Just as Luke started down the hallway a third man came through the garage and straight at him from another hallway. Luke grabbed him. The man elbowed him in the eye, but Luke didn't flinch. He maneuvered him and pulled his back to his chest, and wrapped his arms around his neck. The man was asleep in seconds.

Luke hightailed it back to the library and motioned to the window, holding up two fingers to tell Kyle how many forms of trouble remained in the house.

They were out of the window by the time the two men rushed the room, and out of sight in a flash. Ten minutes later, they climbed into Luke's truck that he'd parked discreetly down the road.

"Well?" Luke asked.

"Empty."

"Of course," Luke said, pulling onto the road. "And we lost our chance to dig around elsewhere."

"Looks like Arel doesn't trust the judge or he wanted whatever the judge owes him in artwork for free."

"Or that Dragonfly person mentioned in the journals wants to cover his ass."

"Or just screw the judge," Kyle suggested. "They're already double-crossing Arel. Why not double-cross each other? We need to figure out who Dragonfly is yesterday."

They did. Kyle was right. "And I need to get Julie out of this today." He couldn't get back to her fast enough.

Chapter Seventeen

Julie worked the crowd in the museum, stopping to chat with a bigwig from a national company, trying to focus on the conversation, but all she could think was, where was Luke? It was the question she'd silently repeated over and over between idle chit-chat. Thinking about a man with a gun waiting on them outside that pizza joint only accelerated her heartbeat, and not with fear for herself. It was the certainty that Luke could easily encounter another man, or men, with weapons.

Julie eased through the crowd again to come face to face with a criminal defense attorney she'd once had a brief fling with, and who had never seemed to learn 'no, means, no." His gaze swept down her body, giving her a lingering inspection.

"Looking amazing as usual, Julie," he said in a suggestive voice, his dark suit fitted to perfection. He was a good looking guy, in an All-American kind of way that seemed to appeal to women, just not to her. Not after he'd become possessive and demanding, which was kind of ironic, since the same qualities in Luke actually turned her on.

"Thank you, Jake," she said. "You do as well. I always have liked your taste in clothes."

He gave her a boyish grin and straightened the blue silk tie at his throat. "You know, I do try to make an impression." His gaze heated and Julie cringed even before he asked, "How about dinner Saturday night? We can go to that little Italian place you like so much."

"I'm afraid all her Saturday nights are otherwise spoken for," a deep voice responded behind her, as a familiar strong hand settled on her back, followed by the jolt his touch always delivered to her senses.

Luke stepped to her side, looking sexier than sin in all black – jacket, shirt, and tie. Alive. Safe. Here with her. And he had a black eye.

Julie reached up to touch it, but Luke flinched and grabbed her hand. "Introduce me to your friend." He put his arm around her waist, possessively pulling her to his side.

Julie felt a strange surge of comfort from the action. Luke wanted Jake and everyone else to know she was with him. If any other man had wanted the same she would have quickly put them in their place. Instead, she just wanted to keep her place by Luke's side.

"Luke, this is Jake," she said, noting how uncomfortable Jake looked and she suddenly felt sorry for him. "He's a master criminal defense attorney, very well respected."

Jake gave Luke's eye a glare. "Looks like you might need one. Perhaps, you'd have been better off staying by your date's side, rather than running into people's fists."

Luke ignored his comment. "Working late isn't high on my list, but certainly necessary at times."

"Appears it was painful as well," Jake added dryly.

Luke shrugged. "You should have seen the other guy." He glanced at Julie. "I think I need a drink." His attention slid briefly back to Jake and he added, "Enjoy your evening," before maneuvering Julie away from him.

Keeping a carefully guarded expression, she whispered to Luke, "Your eye. Are you in pain?" she asked and then added, "And what happened?"

"I'm fine," he assured her, "but it seems we weren't the only ones having a look at Moore's assets, so to speak."

Julie stopped walking and stared up at him. Luke urged her forward with an gentle nudge. "Keep walking, babe. Everything is fine." She let him urge her into a walk again as he added, "If you keep worrying like this I might think you care."

She stopped again, facing him. "I do care, Luke," she said in a voice that trembled. She moved her free hand to his chest. "You know that, right?"

"Yes," he said, softly. "I just wanted to hear you admit it."

She surprised herself, and judging from the look on his face, him, by saying without an ounce of hesitation, "Freely. I admit it freely."

His gaze darkened, heat flaring between them. "I'm going to make you repeat that later tonight, you know? When we're alone."

"Promise?" she asked softly.

"Oh yeah. I promise." He drew her hand into his. "Now, let's skip that drink that was my excuse for getting away from Jake, and get on with our evening."

Suddenly, Julie realized she still didn't know what had happened at Judge Moore's house. "Any luck on that job you were finishing up?" she asked, choosing her wording carefully.

He gave a nod. "Empty," she said. "Any idea where Moore is?"

"I've been great at avoiding him," she said. "But yes. He's back in his display area, beaming over his collection with the guests."

The path to the display hall had several people in the way, all of whom stopped to meet Luke and greet Julie, until finally they entered the hall. The judge was chatting with a young couple and Julie and Luke feigned interest in a painting.

When the couple moved away, the judge immediately greeted Julie. "Ms. Moore. So nice to see you."

"Evening, Judge," she said, as she and Luke met him halfway down the hallway, the only ones remaining in the area. "I'd like you to meet Luke Walker."

"Oh yes, I know your brother, Royce." The judge extended his hand. "Nice to meet you. How'd you score that black eye?"

Luke shook his hand. "My work isn't always easy, but it is always profitable. I believe you'll find that's where myself and my brothers are different breeds."

The Judge's eyes narrowed ever so slightly. "Oh, really? How's that?"

"Well," Luke laughed, flicking a quick look at Julie. "I have a taste for blondes. He prefers brunettes."

Julie frowned, despite the plan underway, and the role she had to play.

"And good taste indeed," the Judge said, glancing at Julie and then back to Luke.

"Hey," she said, doing as she was supposed to, and acting out a bit. "I am here, you two. Stop talking about me like I'm not."

Luke wrapped his arm around her, tugging her to his side a little too roughly. "Behave, sweetheart," he said in a tone that was sharp and unfamiliar, "you know I hate it when you act out in public."

She looked up at him, barely managing the wimpy girl routine. "I'm sorry, Luke, I just–" There was a flash of warning in his eyes that the judge was meant to see before she zipped her lips and then added, "I'll make it up to you later."

Luke kissed her forehead as if he was rewarding a child for correcting poor behavior. "Good girl." Then he turned his attention back to the Judge. "I hear we have a mutual interest."

The Judge was looking at the pair with a dumbfounded expression, like he didn't know Julie any more than she did herself. But that was the idea. She was supposed to come off as someone different, someone he was to believe was the real woman beneath the tough attorney that Luke had the power to expose and manipulate.

"Is that so?" Judge Moore asked of his and Luke's mutual interests, looking at Luke with a little more interest now. "What exactly would that be?"

"I have a knack for getting my hands on unique pieces of art that," he hesitated, "shall we say, others could not. According to your ex-wife, so do you."

"Luke!" Julie exclaimed, as planned. "I told you not to repeat that. I'm sorry, Judge. I'm very sorry. I just...I-"

The Judge's eyes went wide for a split second before a carefully placed mask slipped across his features. "I'm not certain I know what it is you're talking about."

Luke eyed Julie. "Run along, doll. Let us men talk."

"Luke—"

He pulled her close and kissed her. "Run. Along."

She wet her lips. "Okay." She turned and headed down the hall, her stomach in knots. Please let this plan work.

***

"Interesting," the Judge said, watching Julie walk away. "How'd you take such a feisty one like that and make her heel?"

"Secret submission fantasy," he said. "The best kind, in my opinion."

"Indeed," he agreed, narrowing his eyes and seeming to test Luke, by adding. "Who wouldn't want to dominate that fine piece of ass."

Luke gritted his teeth, barely contained the urge to jack the guy against the wall. "And she's useful. She has a powerful client list that suits my, shall we say, interests."

"Meaning what?"

"I cater to special requests. I could be quite useful to the right people."

"Useful?"

"For example, if someone thought to get their hands on a unique piece of art that would otherwise be impossible to obtain, I could make it happen."

The Judge laughed, short and abrupt. "If you're saying what I think you're saying, I'm not buying it. Your brother just married Lauren Reynolds who's a damn prosecutor for the state."

"Interesting that," Luke said. "They have no idea why I really came home. Lauren has put me in the path of a few people I might not have otherwise met."

"And Julie? What does she know?"

"How to please me," he said, with a lift of his lips. "Let me know if you decide you have any special requests." He started to turn. "And by the way, Judge. I did some digging. I know you have an offshore account and I know how much you've deposited into it. I want to work for whoever you're working for. If you're smart, you'll introduce me. I might even throw in a little something special for your private collection, hmm? If not, it would be interesting to see your sweet setup spiral horribly out of control." He turned and sauntered away.

The instant Luke was out of the corridor, Julie was by his side. "Well?"

"He's panicking right now," he said, taking her hand. "Let's go the bar and give him a chance to pick himself up off the floor and decide what to do next."

A few minutes later, they leaned on the bar and Julie sipped champagne. "You know," she said. "I'm going to make you pay for that 'good girl' comment back there."

His lips curved as he repeated the question she'd asked him earlier. "Promise?"

She smiled, a miracle considering her nerves were still in tiny, tight knots. "Oh yes. I promise."

He laughed, low, deep, and sexy. "Sweetheart, I'll pay any way you like."

She eased closer. "Whips and chains?"

He arched a brow. "A new side to you I should know about?"

"Drastic measures to remind you that your submissive little mouse isn't submissive at all."

"I can't wait," he said with a grin, and set her drink down, drawing her hand into his, "but for now, be a good girl and follow along with me. I want to make sure the judge knows just how deep I am in his world. Let's walk."

They spent the next hour feigning interest in random conversations throughout the room, until a waiter appeared with a champagne tray.

"None for me," Julie said automatically.

The waiter looked at Luke, "A message, sir."

Luke reached for a glass and the note laying with it. The man nodded to Luke before moving through the crowd. Luke tucked the note in his pocket.

"Go check on whoever you need to check on," Luke said in a clipped tone as he covertly checked out the room to see if anyone was watching them. "And then we're leaving. Can you do it in fifteen minutes?" They'd already planned this. Luke didn't want her here late, when the crowd thinned and she was an easier target. She was right on board with that.

"Yes," she said, wondering if her heart could take much more of this night. "That's plenty." She rushed away, checking on the closing team, thankful that Elizabeth had one heck of a volunteer team, many of whom Julie knew from past events.

***

Luke didn't look at the note in the museum for a reason. He didn't want to seem eager. The valet brought the truck to the door and Luke helped Julie inside.

Once they were in his truck, he still didn't read it, afraid of watchful eyes. And they were being watched, he was sure of it.

At the first red light they came to he yanked the note from his pocket and unfolded it. He read in silence. Then he cursed running a hand through his hair.

"What?" Julie asked urgently.

Luke tucked the note back into his pocket, and then tugged his tie loose. He flicked a quick look her direction before refocusing on the road.

"I need to think before I can talk about this."

"What does that mean? Luke, please. Tell me what's going on."

"It means I need to think. Give me a minute." His tone was clipped, something she wasn't used to from him and he knew it, but he wasn't himself. In fact, he was someone else who made a stupid mistake that got people killed.

"Luke—"

"It says there's a house party on Staten Island Friday night. The exact location to be disclosed later."

"And you're invited."

His tone was clipped. "Yes." He could feel her attention, her need for more.

"What aren't you telling me?"

"I'm not going."

She was silent a long moment, as if she was trying to read his mind, understand him. When she spoke, the anger was gone from her tone. "But you said children are dying and this was what you wanted?"

"Not only are children dying," he said. "The one agent that was inside is now missing."

"I still don't understand what you're telling me here."

"There are conditions to the invitation that make the risk too high. The end."

He felt her confusion, but for the fifteen-minute ride until he pulled his truck under the Walker building, and into the parking lot, she didn't press him. He killed the engine and sat there, unmoving, staring into the darkness.

She touched his sleeve. "Luke? Talk to me."

He let out a heavy breath and forced his gaze to hers. "My invitation is contingent on you coming with me."

He watched her eyes go wide, the shock slide over her features. "I...see. Why would he want me there?"

"Perhaps to test me. To see if they pass you around I'll flinch. These people are bastards who only want to deal with other bastards. It's all part of their manipulation tactics."

"Can you stop them from...passing me around?"

"We aren't taking a chance that will happen at all. I'm not going. You're not going."

"This is bigger than both of us," she said. "You know that or this wouldn't be eating you alive. We have to do this."

He pulled her to him. "I said no. You are not going." His mouth closed down on hers, hot and demanding. He would not risk her life. He would not let anything happen to her. Luke wasn't sure what happened to him then. He wasn't someone to lose control, but he did now.

Luke had her flat on the seat, her soft curves beneath him, the thick ridge of his shaft pressed between her thighs in a matter of seconds. And he kissed her. God, he couldn't stop kissing her. He thought of Blake, of his brother losing the woman he loved, of the danger of losing Julie. Love. He loved this woman. His mouth trailed down her neck, then lower, to the trim of her dress over her breasts. His hand inched up her dress.

"Do you," she panted, "know how terrified I was for you tonight?"

"Then you know," he said, pulling down her top to tease her nipples, and kissing his way back to her mouth, "why I'm not letting anything happen to you." His mouth closed over hers, and the craving for her, the burn, seemed to expand. His hand slid under her and he lifted her hips, settling more fully in the warm heat he wanted to lose himself in. He had to have her. Here. Now. This instant.

A loud knock sounded on the window.

Chapter Eighteen

Luke looked up to find Hendrix staring at them from the window, and every instinct in him screamed with warning. Luke knew right then that he didn't trust the man. Not even a little bit.

"Give us a minute," he said, fighting the urge that told him to go for his gun. His brother appeared where Hendrix had just been. "Jezus," Luke added. "I said give us a damn minute."

"I'm not alone," Blake called. "Just thought you would want to know."

"Like we don't know that already," Luke mumbled under his breath and tugged at the top of Julie's dress. "Our peeping Tom was one of the task force members. I'm sorry. I don't know what got into me. I knew we'd have a parade chasing us tonight."

"It got into me too, Luke," Julie said, telling him that despite the hellish situation, she was with him for the good and the bad. It was something he wanted to deserve, to own, and not make her regret.

"This is so embarrassing," Julie said. She sat up and reached for her coat where she'd slid out of it back at the valet area.

He adjusted her dress where a little too much of her breast remained in view. "Don't be. You're beautiful, and they're just going to be jealous it was me and not them."

"That doesn't help," she said in a hoarse voice. "Not when we were just talking about men passing me around."

He pulled her close. "That won't happen. Ever. I won't let it." He kissed her temple and motioned to the door. "Let's get this over with."

Luke pushed the truck's door open and walked around to help Julie out. Once he brought her into view, she sat there for a minute not moving. He held out his hand in encouragement. "Come on," he said softly. "Who cares what these guys think?"

She inhaled and let it out before sliding from the vehicle to stand by his side. He took one look at her swollen lips, now lipstick free, the whisker burn on her delicate skin, and knew no one would doubt what they had been doing.

With a sigh he stepped forward, pulling her coat tightly around her, and brushed his lips over hers. They walked toward the stairwell to find Blake waiting, and he wasn't kidding about not being alone. Murphy and Hendrix were with him, which was expected, considering they'd known his plan. That made his losing control in the truck all the more out-of-character.

"Both from the task force," Luke told Julie when she cast him a questioning look.

She gave a barely there nod. "Nothing like making an impression."

"They need to worry about that far more than you do."

"You don't like them?" she asked softly.

"I don't know them well enough to say."

They stopped several feet from the group and Luke quickly introduced Julie. "Why don't I meet you all in the office after I take Julie upstairs?" he suggested. He didn't want her in on this talk. These guys wanted to catch Arel. He wanted to protect Julie. Those two things didn't necessarily coincide. Talking through the evening's events with Julie present wasn't going to work either. She'd put herself at risk, when he wasn't going to let that happen.

She shook her head and crossed her arms, clearly digging in her heels, and proving Hendrix and Murphy were the least of Luke's worries.

"Forget it, Luke. You aren't going to play bodyguard and send me on my way." She let her gaze scan the other men. "Luke was given an invitation to a party on Friday night we assume is to meet Arel. The condition is that I go along with him."

Blake cursed and ran a hand through his hair. "No. That's not happening." His gaze collided with Luke's. "Tell me you didn't agree to this."

"I didn't even consider it," Luke confirmed. "She's not doing it." He cut his attention to Julie. "You aren't doing it."

"You had a tail tonight," Hendrix said. "You're being followed. You're being watched. You're both in this and there isn't an easy exit. You might as well do what you can to save a few innocent kids' lives."

It was a taunt, a way to manipulate Julie, and Luke lost it. He lunged at the son-of-a-bitch, grabbing his coat. Hendrix's phone flew off of his belt and hit the pavement.

"Luke, no!" Julie screamed.

Blake grabbed Luke and shoved him back, getting between him and Hendrix.

Blake pointed at Murphy. "I suggest you get Hendrix out of here before I help Luke beat his ass."

Hendrix grabbed his cell phone from the ground and glared at Luke. "My ass is on the line for letting you in on this. Stop thinking with your dick, man. My ass isn't going down for you." He headed for his SUV in a slow saunter that only had Luke ready to go after him again. Murphy saw it too, walking backward and watching Luke, while Blake stood in front of him, his hand on Luke's chest.

"Don't, Luke," Blake said. "He's a tricky bastard who might just get you thrown in jail."

"He needs me too damn much for that."

Julie stepped up beside Blake. "Don't go after him," she said softly. "Please. I'm begging you, Luke. Don't do it."

That plea wore him down and all the adrenaline pumping through his veins evaporated. His shoulders slowly relaxed. Blake stepped away and let them have space.

"Let's go upstairs," Luke said softly.

"Yes," she said, holding his stare. "I think that would be a very good idea."

It was an announcement of war, but this one war he intended to win. The minute she was inside his apartment, he pulled her into his arms and kissed her, taking her mouth with a hot demand, and when she whimpered, he picked her up and carried her toward the bedroom.

She must have sensed how on edge he was and how out of control he felt He was certain that the only way to feel better was with her, to be inside her, and a part of her, because she didn't argue. She didn't try to talk through what had just happened in the garage.

He stripped her naked and barely remembered undressing himself. He just knew he took her down onto the bed, unable to stop kissing her. He spread her legs and pressed his fingers inside her, craving her soft sounds of pleasure. Craving her. And when she came, when she moaned with release, he only wanted more. He needed more.

Luke pulled her beneath him, settling into the slick, wet heat of her body. And then he was inside her, with her. Her skin was soft, her kisses sweet and sultry, her responses to his touch intensely erotic.

She moaned and arched into him, clinging to him, as if she felt what he did, as if she was standing on a ledge with him, the only thing keeping him from falling.

They clung to each other and moved together as if they were trying to become one, until she spasmed around him and took him over the edge with her. They collapsed together. Time ticked by in silence until their breathing evened out.

Until Julie said, "Luke—"

"Don't say it," he said, pressing his forehead to hers. "You're not going. I'll find another way."

"What if you can't?"

"I will." Because he had to. Because he wasn't letting anything happen to her.

***

Gina threw her purse down on the kitchen counter as she entered her apartment, disgusted from thinking about how Julie had floated around the museum, being complimented by everyone. They all loved Julie at that party, and what was Gina? Her assistant. Her fucking assistant.

Marco came up behind her and wrapped his arms around her. "What's wrong, bebe?"

She turned in his arms. "Even you wanted her," she accused. "I saw how you looked at her."

"I looked at her," he said, not even asking who she meant, because he knew. "I touch you."

"Not tonight you won't." She tried to push away from him, but those big strong arms of his held her, one big hand molding her closer.

"I know what you need," he claimed softly, that damnable sexy accent of his tingling along her nerve endings. "Something special to make you forget how much you hate this woman you work for."

"I don't want to forget." She wanted to remember. Oh yes, she wanted to remember, and she wanted to do something about it.

He slipped a feather light strip of something to her lips and she frowned as it began to melt, pulling back. "What is that?"

"A new kind of pleasure," he promised. "You will feel me in ways you never thought possible."

She didn't do drugs. It had always been her taboo. She didn't like feeling out of control. But whatever he'd given her began to dissolve on her lips and instinct made her scrape it with her teeth, the sweetness of it drawing a swipe of her tongue.

"That's it, ma belle," he approved, and pressed more of the sliver of sweetness into her mouth and this time she accepted it willingly. It was good and he was just so damn convincing without even trying.

Suddenly she felt warm and wonderful, and wait, was she on the bed? How had she gotten on the bed? And where were her clothes? Not that she cared. Naked was good. Naked with Marco was even better. Her world was spinning, but in rainbow colors where time and space seemed some distant place. Marco was nowhere, yet he was everywhere, kissing her, whispering naughty, wonderful things to her.

"You hate Julie, oui?" he asked by her ear, and his hand was on her stomach, heat seeping into her skin and sending these amazing sensations through her.

"Yes, I hate her." She rolled over and wrapped her arms around him but then she blinked and everything went blank. She couldn't remember what she'd said but she was pretty sure that, oh wow, oh, yes....she'd just had the orgasm of orgasms. "Do it again," she demanded. "Make me come again."

"Non," he declined, his lips on her neck. "Not until you give me something. Remember? That's how we play this game. I give you pleasure. You give me...something. Now, tell me more about this journal."

"The journal," she whispered, trying to remember why she hadn't told him about it before now. Wasn't there a reason? She couldn't think of the reason. This was Marco, the man who made her feel so good, the man she wanted to be rich and naked with for the rest of her life. "The judge," she whispered, pressing his hand to her breast. "He will pay for it."

"How much?"

"I don't know...I thought fifty thousand...." Rainbows floated in her vision again and she blinked them away. "I think much more."

"And where," he said, against her mouth, "is this journal?"

"Julie has it."

Chapter Nineteen

I t was early Friday morning, the day of the party, and Luke had yet to get instructions about where to go and when. He sat at a coffee shop several tables from where Julie was meeting with a client, his MacBook open. She'd called in with the flu for two days, and then worked twelve-hour days from his office. Today though, she insisted she had to go by her office for a meeting and to pick up some files. He planned to wait on her in the building.

Luke's cell rang and he snatched it from his belt and grimaced at Murphy's number. "Why do I know this is you trying to convince me to take Julie to Arel's party?"

"I've studied this guy for two years," Murphy said. "He's got the same mentality gangs operate with. The strong get respect and rise to the top. The weak are destroyed. You told the judge you use Julie to get to her high-powered clients. If the judge shared that information, which considering he's trying to stay on Arel's good side, I'd venture that he did, then Arel will want the power you have by the impression that you basically own Julie."

"So he wants her."

"He wants the power and the control," Murphy said. "You make damn sure he knows that she's yours and hands off. Be good to you, and he'll get rewarded through you."

"Great information," Luke said, "but nothing I'm going to put to use tonight."

"Two more dead teens last night in Jersey," he said. "We have to shut them down." He hesitated. "That missing agent we told you about."

"Yes?"

"She had two sisters, a brother, and a fiancé. Her name is Lauren Michael. She likes cheese pizza and can eat more than any of us guys, but she's a tiny little thing. She reads romance novels, but is still tougher than sin, and handles a gun better than most men. Oh, and her father was killed by a drugged-up dude on the street for the twenty bucks he had in his pocket. Bring her home, Luke." The line went dead.

Luke held the phone to his forehead. Damn it. Damn it to hell. Think man. Think your way out of this. He cut a sideways look at Julie, an ache in his heart just looking at her. She trusted him to keep her safe and he couldn't fail.

"Mister?"

Luke looked up to find a kid not more the twelve standing beside him. The kid shoved an envelope at him. Luke accepted it. "Who's it from."

He shrugged. "I don't know him but he gave me a hundred bucks." He took off for the door.

Luke ripped open the card.

If you want to work with me, you need to know the price of crossing me. I can get to you, or your playmate, or your brothers, or anyone I damn well please, any time, any place. Be at the Staten Island Ferry waiting for pick-up at eight sharp and bring Ms. Harrison.

Luke inhaled deeply, the sound of Julie's voice as she and her client stood up and shook hands catching his attention. He slid the note into his briefcase and shut his computer.

She walked over to him and sat down, hanging her briefcase on the chair. "Did you hear the news? About the two dead teenagers?"

With grim acceptance of where this was leading, he gave a nod. "I heard."

"I have to go with you," she said. "I have to."

Luke knew he'd been backed into a corner, that he had a choice to make and make quickly. He could kidnap her and hide her away someplace safe. She'd hate him, but she wouldn't be dead. Or he could do something that might also make her hate him, but would keep her alive, as well.

"I got a call today," he said. "I'm to be at the Staten Island Ferry at eight tonight, alone. Seems Arel didn't agree with the judge's guest list."

She studied him long and hard, seeing way too much. "You're trying to protect me, aren't you?"

Her cell phone rang in her hand and she sighed. "It's Gina. It might be about my meeting that I pray is cancelled." She answered the call and listened a moment.

"Okay," she finally said. "I'll swing by there. I'm close anyway. Tell the partners I might be a few minutes late to the meeting." She hung up. "Gina's purse was stolen. She has a key to my apartment from cat-sitting and thought I should have my locks changed. I'm only two blocks from here. I want to swing by and check on things and tell the doorman."

***

Luke's bad feeling got worse when they arrived at Julie's building to find the power was off, and the doorman had his hands full calming tenants and trying to get answers.

He and Julie walked the stairs and when they got to her floor, he took her key and unlocked the door. He held her back and shoved the door open. Everything she owned had been destroyed. The walls were spray-painted, her couches shredded.

"Oh God," Julie gasped, holding onto the wall. "Who would do this?"

"Call the police," Luke said, pulling his gun from his pants and heading inside. "I'll look around."

Luke found her bedroom in the same shape as the rest of the place but what really struck him as odd was her clothes had been all cut up.

He headed back to the hallway to find Julie just hanging up with the police. "They're on their way."

"Everything you own is shredded," he said. "Even your clothes."

She took a deep breath and leaned on the wall. "I can't believe this is happening."

"I'd say what happened in there was out of hatred, and that Gina is a good suspect, but that seems too obvious."

"What are you saying?"

"Someone might want that journal," he said. "And if they know Gina hates you, then she's a perfect cover."

"I didn't even know she hated me," she argued.

"Which means it has to be someone intimate with Gina. And someone smart enough to cut the power so the cameras wouldn't be working."

"The judge, maybe?" Julie asked.

"Maybe."

"But haven't you been watching him?"

"We have him under surveillance," he said. "But we could have missed something before we were fully operational. Calls could be made from disposable phones or lines we don't have access to. There are three people we know of that would want the journal. The judge, this Dragonfly person, and Arel, if he knows it exists."

"You think he does?"

"You never underestimate a man like Arel." Which was why Luke wasn't taking Julie with him to the party.

"There's no way out of this, is there?" she asked. "We're in too deep with too many bad people."

"Hey now," he said, wrapping her in his arms. "That's not true. They want the journal, not you."

"They tried to kill us by the pizza place, Luke. They think I – we – know what's in it, and we do."

"We'll take down the judge and we'll get Dragonfly," he promised.

"You don't even know who Dragonfly is."

"No," he said. "But Arel does and I'll hand him the journal if that's what it takes to make sure Dragonfly doesn't come at us in our sleep."

"And Arel? He runs a cartel, Luke."

Luke replayed the note in his head. It had clearly come directly from Arel, not the judge. I can get to you, or your playmate, or your brothers, or anyone I damn well please, any time, any place.

***

Late Friday, Julie sat at Luke's kitchen table, working on some files while he was downstairs in his office planning out the night's visit to the cartel's party. She'd skipped her meeting, or rather missed it, as the police asked a million questions to which Luke had her give generic replies. Any mention of a journal, the judge, or the cartel had been avoided. She was rattled but the scary disaster that was her apartment paled in comparison to her worries over the danger Luke would be in tonight. Her staying behind didn't make her feel better. In fact, it made her feel like everything was spinning out of control.

She settled her elbows on the table and pressed her fingers to her temples. There was a reality here she had to face. Yes, Luke could deal with the judge and Dragonfly by simply handing them to Arel. But they were in deep with a cartel, and getting out, and taking down Arel, meant Luke had to do something an entire task force had been trying to do and failed.

She googled cartels, and started reading stories about undercover agents, about the murders and the ruined lives, and was halfway through one that gave her some hope, when her computer died. She jiggled her cord and still nothing, and that was when she realized it had an exposed wire.

Pushing to her feet, she knew she needed a new cord, but for now, she'd borrow Luke's. She was pretty sure she'd seen his computer case in the hallway. Julie headed that way and found it on the entry table. She unzipped it and found the cord, and pulled out a note card with it. It fluttered to the ground and she squatted down to grab it, and then went utterly still as she read the text.

If you want to work with me, you need to know the price of crossing me. I can get to you, or your playmate, or your brothers, or anyone I damn well please, any time, any place. Be at the Staten Island Ferry waiting for pick up at eight sharp and bring Ms. Harrison.

Her lashes lowered and emotions overwhelmed her. He was planning to go alone, knowing the increased danger to himself. She couldn't let that happen. And wasn't she just facing the facts? If Arel didn't go down she was either going into hiding, or dying. Julie pushed to her feet. She wasn't doing either while Luke put his life on the line. She'd brought him into this. She was going to do everything, even risk her life, to get him out of this. He'd lied but she knew it was to protect her, and she'd go along with his story. She knew where to be and at what time.

Chapter Twenty

The task force is already on Staten Island?" Julie asked. She sat on Luke's bed and he was beside her, inserting some sort of tracking device into the heel of his boot. He wore all black again, and she knew it was to blend into the shadows if he had to escape the cartel. Would it be too obvious if she did as well?"

"And our team," he said. "Blake left earlier this afternoon. Jesse will be here in a few minutes to stay with you. Do what he says. He'll protect you."

So she'd have to get past Jesse. She should have assumed such a problem would exist. "Can you take a weapon?"

He flipped the boot he held around and showed her the switchblade latched inside. "It's small but it'll get the job done if I need it."

"There will be many of them and one of you, Luke," she worried.

"And I hope it makes them underestimate me." He flipped the heel to his boot into place and put it on. "And with the tracking device, if I leave the house, my team will know."

"Just like Arel will know you were a SEAL. He'll know to be cautious."

He turned to her and covered her hand with his. "I might not be in the SEALs any longer, sweetheart, but I'm still a SEAL. I'm going to go in there and do what I have to in order to protect the innocent people the cartel is hurting."

She read between the lines and knew he meant he'd die if he had to. Though she knew she'd see him soon, part of her feared he'd slip away and she'd never see him again. Julie pressed her mouth to his, her fingers curling at his jaw, repeating a version of what she had said to him once years before. "Stay alive. The world needs more good men like you."

And just like in the past, he tightened his arm around her waist, and asked, "And what do you need?"

"You," she whispered. "I need you."

He kissed her, a kiss that ravished her with passion and intensity. When he pulled away, his eyes dark and turbulent, he vowed, "I'll see you by morning." Then he was gone.

Julie heard Luke speaking to Jesse in the other room and she knew she had no time to waste if she was going to make it on that ferry. The instant she heard the door and the television come on, she grabbed a robe and pulled it over her sweats before headed to the living room.

"Hey, Jesse," Julie said, walking into the living room. "I'm just going down to Lauren's place to get some bubbles for a bath and try on some clothes. I have nothing left and I want to bring a few things back over here."

He stood up. "I'll go with you."

"No, no, please don't. This place is, as Luke says, like Fort Knox, and...well. A few minutes alone, doing girl stuff would help me right now. I'm frankly trying not to have a meltdown over Luke going to the party."

"He's going to be okay," he assured her.

She hugged herself. "Thanks, but I might have that meltdown if we talk about this. Believe me. A little girl primping will do me good. Then, how would you feel about ordering pizza? I always eat pizza when I'm stressed. Will that be some security breach?"

"Pizza is good," he said. "Worth risking my life for."

She laughed. He was a nice guy, and way too good looking for the single female population's well being. She wasn't one of them though, not anymore.

"I won't be long," she said. "Okay. I might be a bit. When I start with the clothes...well, you know."

"Yes," he said. "I have two sisters. I know."

Julie kept her pace slow as she made her way to the door, but the instant she was in the hallway she took off running for Lauren's door. She was in a flash and rushing for the bedroom, where she ripped open the closet and grabbed the hot pink dress she'd tried on earlier in the day. As much as black tempted her, she was supposed to be Luke's 'playmate' and that meant arm candy. Besides, she was curvier than Lauren and finding a dress that fit was a struggle. She slid the silk over her hips and grimaced the unavoidable cleavage, she refused to think about. The idea of becoming the playmate of everyone at the party was not something she could consider. This was about Luke, and innocent kids, and it mattered, like he mattered. She was doing this because it was the right thing to do.

She shoved on her black heels she'd worn earlier for work, grabbed her purse she'd left here, and made tracks to the door. Her coat was next door and Lauren's were too small so she was just going to have to freeze. Pausing, she inhaled and willed her nerves to calm, before slowly exhaling. She had to be quiet. She had to make this happen. She dug out the truck key she'd swiped from Luke's key ring when she'd heard he was taking a cab, to avoid his truck being tampered with when he was on the island.

She kicked off her heels and picked them up and cautiously, silently, opened the door. And then she took off running, heading down the hall and then the stairs. She exited the garage door and shoved her feet in her shoes, and ran for Luke's truck. She could barely breathe, and her hand was shaking as she unlocked the doors and inserted the key. She backed up and drove for the exit, using the remote above Luke's visor and keying in the three digit code she'd seen him use. Once she cleared the doors, she prayed for light traffic. At the first stoplight, she grabbed her cell phone and punched the auto-dial for Jesse. Luke had put it in her phone, along with Blake's and Kyle's.

He answered on the first ring. "Anything wrong?"

She sighed. "No. I just didn't want you to worry. I decided to take a hot bath and it's a little piece of heaven. Will you starve to death if I linger a bit?"

"No," he said. "I'll just raid Luke's kitchen. You do whatever you have to do to be okay tonight."

"Thank you, Jesse. I'm really sorry you got babysit the girlfriend duty."

"Hey," he said. "I have SportsCenter and a pizza in my future. Life is good."

Julie ended the call with a little more small talk. You do whatever you to do to be okay. It seemed like a good plan. She was going to be okay and so was Luke. They had to be.

***

Somehow, Julie made it to the ferry by with fifteen minutes to spare. Luke was leaving on the 8:00 ferry and she could only hope there was only one leaving at this hour. She rushed towards the terminals, thankful the ride was free because she wouldn't have had time to buy a ticket. Bingo. One ferry for the nine o'clock trip but the terminal was packed. She had to be aggressive enough to be one of the people on the boat.

Julie pushed through the crowd, enduring many a shove to find her way to the semi-front of the mass of people, just as the gates opened. She held her breath until she stepped onto the boat and then took off for the back of the vehicle, and an inner cabin where it was warm. She headed to the bathroom, where she could hide so Luke wouldn't see her until the boat started to move.

A bad thought hit her though as the horn sounded, warning that they were about to depart. What if he wasn't on the boat? Oh god. She pulled out her cell and dialed his number only to get no signal. Panicked she opened the bathroom door to find Luke standing there, having obviously followed her, and the look on his face said he was furious.

Without a word, he gripped her arm and started pulling her toward the cabin exit, ignoring the people who were watching them.

"Luke, damn it. Stop pulling me."

"When you're off this boat, I'll stop," he said, not looking at her. "Not a second sooner."

***

Luke cursed as the gates lowered and Julie was trapped on the boat. He turned to her, so furious he could barely speak.

"I've before never in my life wanted to put a woman over my knee and spank her, but you're testing me."

"Try it and see where my knee lands."

"I told you the invitation was for me and me alone."

She snorted. "That's not what it said when I found it in your bag."

His cell phone started to ring and he knew who it was even before he flipped it open. "Jesse, you fool," he growled into the phone. "She's here on the damn boat with me and I'm going to kick your ass when I get back there. Get someone on the other side waiting on her to take her back."

She started to walk away. Luke ended the call, grasping her wrist and pulling her close. "You're not staying."

"Try to send me away and I swear to you, Luke, that I'll make such a scene we'll both end up at the police station."

"You'd blow this and have me arrested?" he challenged.

"Yes," she said, the wind lifting her hair as the boat began to move, the engine and the horn drowning out anything else she might say.

Luke pulled her with him inside a car, where he didn't stop until they were in the back, away from everyone. He urged her down into the seat next to him, and shrugged out of his leather jacket when he realized she was shivering. He wrapped it around her, and holding the lapels, turned her to face him.

"You shouldn't be here."

"When you asked if I'd get you arrested rather than be sent home, I said yes. And you know why? Because we both know you have a better chance of getting out of this alive with me present. I won't let you die because I stayed home when you needed me."

His chest felt like it might explode. "I can't let you do this."

"You said never underestimate Arel, so assume he already knows I'm here. I assume he saw us fighting, and think about the image you've portrayed of controlling me. Then kiss me into submission."

Luke took that in and did exactly what she suggested. He kissed her, and he made it look as good as it felt. He kissed her and he slid his hand under her coat and pulled her close. She was right. He had painted a portrait and she'd just given him the way to send her home. She'd disobeyed him and she'd been sent home to wait for her punishment. Arel would buy it, especially if they were being watched. And there was no question that they were.

Luke tore his mouth from hers. "So, you'll be my good girl and do exactly as I say. Play the game and everything will be just fine."

"I will," she promised.

Good, he thought, because when he scolded her and ordered her to go home in front of Arel's men, she'd have no choice but to do as he said, or get him killed.

Chapter Twenty-One

Luke couldn't get Julie out of here fast enough. He held Julie close as they headed for the exit of the ferry, ready to break through the ground and hand her off. By the time they were on the street and he was looking for one of his men, a black town-car pulled up in front of them. Immediately, a burly man in a dark suit got out.

"Good evening, Mr. Walker," he said, and then inclined his head at Julie, "Ms. Harrison." He opened the back door. "Please enjoy your ride to the party."

Luke didn't move. "Actually, Ms. Harrison will be returning to the city. We've had a...disagreement I'd prefer to deal with when we're alone."

Julie gasped and turned to him. "Luke," she said, and surprised him by sliding right into her role, "I promised I'd behave and I will. I was just upset about riding separately to the ferry and forgetting my coat."

"You're both to come," the said. "No deviation allowed." His eyes met Luke's. "Not if you want Mr. Arel's business." He lifted his coat just enough to make sure it was clear how far he'd go to get them in the car. "And just so you know, Arel gets rather cranky when someone turns down his invitations." In other words, Julie came with them or she'd be killed. The man dropped the jacket and motioned them forward. "Shall we?"

Where there was one gun, there were more, and probably pointed at them, waiting to take a shot. Luke motioned Julie into the car, wishing her dress showed a little less leg as she climbed inside.

The instant she was safely out of view, Luke's gaze lifted to the man's, and Luke knew he was in a bad spot. He looked weak by letting Julie go along. He risked them both being killed, if he did not. Everything was a test: they either survived or failed and died. Luke didn't intend to fail or die.

Before the man could blink again, Luke grabbed the man's wrist and reached for the gun, sliding his hand to the handle without removing it. "Be glad I want to meet your boss because I don't like being disrespected in front of my woman, or anyone for that matter." He released the man. "This stays between us, unless you give me a reason to consider you a liability. At which time I will hunt you down and kill you and tell your boss I got rid of his weak link."

As soon as he slid inside, he could almost feel the fear rolling off of Julie, and it wasn't going to serve either of them well. He needed to come off confident and comfortable, and Julie couldn't let her fear show. He pulled Julie close and slid her hand to his leg.

"So, what are you going to do to make me glad I brought you along."

"What do you want me to do?"

Nothing in front of the driver and the man who'd just recovered from wetting himself and slid into the front passenger seat, but it wasn't that easy.

Luke kissed her, his hand sliding up her leg. They were going to put on a show, and show as little as possible in the process.

***

Twenty minutes later, they pulled up to a beachfront mansion that Luke would bet was used for entertainment, but wouldn't be Arel's actual home. No, Arel would not be stupid enough to live where he entertained. Water worked for him. He liked it, he could live with it, but with Julie by his side, it wasn't a good escape route.

The door opened and the same man who invited them into the car waved them out. Luke stepped out of the car, ignoring the coldness of the night as he tuned into what was important, even as he offered Julie a hand and helped her to her feet. Discreetly, he took in exit routes, numbers of vehicles, and signs of guards, and location of windows.

Cold wind gusted across the ocean, whipping around Julie's shoulders and she shivered, even with his coat wrapped around her. He wrapped his arm around her, trying to shield her from the force of the gusts until they stepped inside the foyer of the house. Julie shivered and blew on her hands.

"In there," the man said, motioning toward two massive double doors.

Shelves of old books lining an entire wall of the room behind a massive oak desk. To the right of the desk a leather couch and two chairs framed a fireplace. In front of the desk were two chairs, and in front of those, three men, all dressed in black cargo pants, and all wearing shoulder holsters with guns.

One of the men, the tallest of the three with a long blond pony tail and a face that looked like it could stop time, moved forward.

"I'm Michael," he said. "Head of security here. Well be doing a search before you enter the main house," he said, and snapped at Julie, "Coat."

Luke helped Julie remove the jacket, keenly aware of the male attention on her. He handed the jacket to Michael, and when Michael's gaze lingered on Julie's breasts, Luke said, "You want to keep those eyes?"

Michael's attention snapped upward, a smile twitching on his lips that told Luke this one wasn't as easily intimidated as the last.

"Ladies, first," Michael said, glancing at Julie. "Hands on the desk, and spread your legs."

Julie gasped and turned to Luke.

"In your wet dreams, man," Luke said, "but not in this lifetime."

The man arched a brow. "Either I search her or she spends the party here, with me."

He grabbed the coat from the man. "Tell your boss I don't share well with others, but I'm damn good at what I do. When he wants to find out how good, he knows where to find me." He turned, pulling Julie close, only to hear. "Wait."

Slowly, Luke turned around, arching a brow as the other man had only moments before.

"We'll provide a female to pat her down."

Luke still didn't like it, but it was as close to compromise as he suspected they would get. He glanced at Julie and she wet her lips and nodded. Slowly, they turned back around.

"Step forward," the man ordered, clearly the only one of the three allowed to communicate. "We'll search you while we wait on the female, unless you'd prefer to be patted down by a woman yourself?"

"Just the one you wish you could have and can't," Luke said, handing Julie the coat and stepping forward. The other two men stepped to the sides of the desk as Luke planted his hands on the wooden surface and let the asshole pat him down.

When he shoved off the desk and turned, he stood toe to toe with the man and lowered his voice. "Just so we're clear. If you so much as think about fucking her again, I'll rip your balls out through your throat and hand them to your boss." He turned away, as the 'female' who wasn't much of a female at all walked in. Stocky, five foot five, and wearing cargo pants, she was more man than some he knew.

Luke silently cursed as the 'female' sauntered forward, and gave Julie a once over from behind that made him want to backhand the bitch.

Michael motioned the other men out of the room. "I'm staying to protect my guard."

The female guard stepped to Michael's side and Luke could almost feel Julie's discomfort, and the smirk on both Michael and the woman's face said they were enjoying it.

Julie inhaled and let it out. "Let's get this over with." Bravely, she walked forward. Michael and the female stepped aside and Julie planted her hands on the desk.

Chapter Twenty-Two

L uke felt helpless watching the guard grope Julie. He should have protected her. He should have found a way to get her out of this. But it was over, finally over.

When the party motioned toward the door, he pulled her close under his shoulder, and whispered, "I'm going to make this up to you."

She didn't say anything, didn't even look at him, and he knew she was struggling with her feelings, which only made him feel like a bigger dog. But he couldn't think about that now. He had to focus, to make sure he knew how to get them out of here if he had to.

They were led past a set of stairs and into a massive living room with a high ceiling, walls of massive stained-glass windows, and furniture in sleek black leather. A variety of people, all dressed to impress, mingled, Judge Moore included. Several waiters held trays filled with drinks.

Luke glanced around to find the man who'd escorted them up gone, then he refocused on Julie and followed her gaze to the the painting of several sailboats on an ocean over a fireplace.

"That Monét," she whispered, "is supposed to be in a museum in London."

"It's probably a fake," he said, but Luke didn't doubt the real thing was in Arel's possession, thus why he had this one displayed.

"I hope you're right," she said. "Because it's worth a fortune."

Luke's gaze returned to the judge to find he was sitting in a leather chair next to a man who'd not been there moments before. Dressed in an expensive suit, the thirty-something blond male oozed so much arrogant confidence that even if Luke hadn't seen pictures of Arel, he'd have known it was him.

The judge looked up and he and Luke locked gazes. He never even spared Julie a glance. Several seconds ticked by before he leaned in to listen to something Arel said. When the judge looked up again, he motioned to Luke to join them.

"Play the game," he said softly.

"The game from hell," she said, and smiled up at him and jokingly said with a bat of her lashes, "Whatever you say, my lord and master."

"And if I believed that I'd buy up all the swampland and be a millionaire."

She laughed, and it was well timed as they joined the two men. "Judge," Luke said with a nod.

"This is Paul Arel," the Judge replied without acknowledging Luke's greeting. "Your host."

"Bonsoir, Monsieur Walker." He tilted his head toward Luke, but never offered his hand. Turning to Julie, his eyes carefully fixed on her eyes, and not her breasts, he said, "Et Ms. Harrison, tres belle, just as I have heard."

Luke knew why Arel watched her eyes. The eyes were the path to the soul, to your hidden secrets, and he was trying to read her. "Thank you," Julie said. "And I so appreciate the invitation tonight."

"I hope the ride over was comfortable, Julie. You don't mind if I call you Julie, do you? Certainly you may call me Paul."

"The ride was not what was expected," Luke said, ending Arel's attempt to pull down her guard, something he'd never achieve. Julie might be scared, but she was a brilliant attorney, and a smart cookie. "I don't like talking around things. Time is money, and I know you want more of it, as do I. I believe we can find some mutually beneficial ground, but trust needs to be established."

"Ah," Arel said. "Indeed, it does. Why don't you get a drink, and relax a bit. Then we can talk about exactly how my trust might be obtained. It will not be a easy task."

Damn, the man's accent was killing him. Luke looked down at Julie. "Go get us drinks, darlin', and let me talk business."

Julie nodded. "Of course." She started to move and Luke pulled her mouth to his, sliding his tongue against hers, before he added, "Make it quick. I'm feeling rather thirsty all of a sudden."

Her eyes went wide but she nodded and he released her.

Judge Moore stared at Julie's retreating back and laughed in disbelief. "Tell me your secret for making a woman like that submissive."

Luke focused on the judge with a hard stare. "Start with being me, not you."

Arel barked out a laugh while the judge looked like he wanted to throttle Luke. There was growing interest in Arel's attention to Luke. "You have balls, I'll give you that, but do you have brains and stamina?"

Luke's lips twitched. "You'll have to give me trust to find out."

Arel laughed. "Your brothers, they are, as you Americans say...saints? Why should I believe you are not one as well, perhaps in disguise?"

"Because everyone who's supposed to be a saint is, right?" he asked sarcastically, his gaze settling on the judge, and returning to Arel. "I assume you keep him around because his assumed sainthood has come in quite handy?"

Arel didn't reply, his gaze penetrating. "You were a SEAL, non?"

"I was."

"SEALs are—"

"Trained killers," Luke provided.

Arel considered that during another eternal pause. "What is it you feel you can do for me, Monsieur Walker?"

Luke noted the formality. No first names for him. "I have a knack for procuring, shall we say, difficult to find artwork." Luke's gaze moved to the piece above the fireplace. "Much like that one."

Arel let a slow smile slip onto his lips. "You are an interesting man. Still, art is only a sideline interest. I need someone who can be more diverse."

Luke quirked a brow. "I consider everything." He paused and then added, "If the price is right."

Arel's eyes narrowed. "The woman, she has a powerful list of clients. You control her?"

"Completely."

"You can get to anyone she can get to?"

"Yes."

He narrowed his gaze. "You will be tested, Monsieur Walker, and we will start small. See you don't fail. Those who fail me, I don't kill them until they feel great pain."

"I don't fail. Ever. So get on with the test."

"You will be contacted," Arel said, and then with a small smile, added, "Now go enjoy my hospitality, and please feel free to use the upstairs rooms for..." Arel flicked a glance at Julie as she approached. "Tonight should be about money and pleasure." He smiled wickedly. "When you wish to leave, simply tell my driver."

He nodded to Luke, and then waved for the judge to follow him as he stood up started for the door, with the judge on his heels like a whipped pup.

Julie blinked in confusion. "What happened?"

He gave her a tight smile. "It's moving along fine."

Lethally fine, that was.

***

Judge Moore followed Arel into his private office, fighting his growing uneasiness. The room was filled with a large, mahogany desk, plush leather furnishings, and decorated with a vast collection of art. As usual the judge's eyes locked onto the The D'Ambrosi, The Dancer, a bronze 15' statue on a wooden base next to the desk he'd found for Arel. This one was fake, like everything in this place, but Arel had the real work, as he had so many brilliant masterpieces the judge hungered to possess.

Two large brown wing chairs sat in front of a fireplace that sparked red hot. Waving a hand toward the chairs, Arel said, "Let's sit." The chairs were angled toward each other, and the judge knew Arel would be watching him the way he always watched everyone. Looking for anything that was off, any reason to consider someone a threat.

Once they were seated, Arel opened a cigar box sitting on the small table between the two chairs. Arel smelled the cigar. "Ah," he murmured. "So perfect."

He turned the box toward the Judge and waited expectantly for him to remove one. As Judge Moore sniffed the cigar he was aware of several guards entering the room and coming to stand near their backs. Arel often kept men nearby, but something about their silent entrance was bothersome.

Arel lit both of their cigars. Then, he took several puffs of his cigar, taking his time to enjoy it. With each moment of silence, the judge felt his tension rise, bit by bit, until he was ready to come unglued. Carefully, he kept his expression neutral, but his mind raced with possibilities, none of them good.

"So," Arel finally said. "When were you going to tell me about the journal?"

His first inclination was to play dumb. The judge started to speak and Arel held up a hand. "Don't deny what I know already, or you will sadly regret your action, Judge."

The judge swallowed. Hard. He couldn't let Arel have that journal. What if it exposed his activity with Dragonfly? "I have it handled. My wife caused more trouble than I had hoped. I didn't want you to feel I couldn't take care of things."

Arel eyes narrowed. "You didn't take care of things. I did. She might still be a problem had I left you to your own solutions."

He cleared his throat. "That's why I didn't want you to have to deal with this. I knew you would be angry."

Arel smiled, his lips twisting in an evil grin. "I don't get angry."

The judge felt his empty hand tremble and clenched it into a fist. "I have this handled. It's a small problem."

"You, Judge, are the problem. Be careful or you may be one I no longer tolerate. Answer me these questions. Why is Ms. Harrison holding the diary? And why is the sister of the dead wife missing? These things happen, yet you bring me Monsieur Walker. He controls her. He has the journal."

His mind raced and the truth seemed his best defense. "I believe the journal is how he found out about you, yes, and why I thought getting him inside our operation making money would ensure he was loyal. You saw how he controls her. She won't do anything he doesn't want her to do."

"If Monsieur Walker is as good as he seems to be at manipulation, he may want to use it against me at some point."

Arel leaned forward resting his arms on his knees. "Consider this handled as of now. I will resolve it."

"But—"

Arel's hand sliced through the air. "Non! I am done." Then he spoke over his shoulder in French to one of the guards before speaking to the judge again. "You will go with Fredrick. He will remind you why I don't like secrets."

The judge went cold, fear shooting through him at the speed of burning fuel. "Please, no. I won't ever—"

Arel cut him off. "No, you won't." He spoke to the guard in English this time. "Take him."

Two guards grabbed his arms as he struggled. The soft sound of a gun being cocked made him still. The judge looked up.

Arel pointed a small gun at him. "I suggest you walk calmly from the room, perhaps even smile a bit. It would be a pity to dirty my carpet."

With more courage than he felt, the judge said, "You're bluffing. The guests will hear the shot."

"Ah, but that's where you are wrong. A silencer makes this gun the perfect choice, non?"

Marco walked from the shadows of the room and stood next to his brother. Arel stayed focused on the judge as he spoke again to the guards. "Take him away. If he makes even one wrong move, kill him."

One of the guards drove a fist into the judge's stomach making him bend at the waist and grab his middle. They wouldn't kill him, he told himself. They needed him. Slowly, he straightened only to find himself spun around toward the exit door.

The guard, who he knew only as Rodriquez bent toward him, forcing a wave of horrid, sour breath against his cheek. "You heard the man. Smile." He laughed, evil and tauntingly low. "Or else."

Marco looked at his brother as the door shut, leaving them alone. "He's trouble."

"He has been useful," Arel said walking to the cigar box and offering one to Marco.

Marco waved it away. "He needs to be dealt with."

Arel said, "We need him."

"Like a hole in the head, brother," Marco insisted. "He lied. That spells trouble."

Arel lit his cigar and took a long draw. Blowing out the smoke, his expression became resigned. "If you are so certain he's trouble, get rid of him."

Marco started to speak.

"Non," Arel said harshly, changing his mind. "Only after I have the journal, and ensure we don't need him. Then, and only then, are you to dispose of him."

"Brother—"

Arel scowled at Marco. "Enough of this," he said sourly. "Don't you cross me, Marco. "

Marco's voice was low, his expression resolved. "I have never crossed you nor will I now."

Arel was quiet for a minute as if he was deciding whether or not he believed Marco. Abruptly, he smiled. "Good," he said. "Call Dragonfly and set up a test for Monsieur Walker. If he's trying to bust us, Dragonfly will find out. Tell him to come here, tonight."

Marco pulled out his cell phone and made the call. When Marco was done, he joined his brother, sitting down in the chair the judge had occupied. "He'll be here in two hours."

Arel picked up the cigar box and held it open for Marco. "Smoke with me, and tell me about this woman you have been using so effectively, the one who told you about the journal. Shall we dispose of her as well?"

***

As much as Luke wanted to get the hell out of Dodge, if they left too soon, Arel would be suspicious. So he forced himself to mingle with the guests, thankful for Julie's ability to talk to people, and proud of her for how smooth she was under pressure. What was the most shocking, with guards at the door, was how many of the guests seemed oblivious to the true career of their host, thinking him some type of investor they all used for brokering deals. Impatiently, Luke waited to make his exit until Arel and the judge returned, certain they would. It was nearly an hour before Arel returned without the judge.

Then and only then, and when he knew that Arel was watching them, did Luke pull Julie close and kiss her, and then head for the hallway. He led her down the hallway and into a corner near the kitchen entrance and leaned against the wall, pulling her soft curves against his body, and wrapping his arms around her.

He nuzzled her ear, skimming his hand across the soft curve of her neck. "What are you doing, Luke?" she demanded in a husky whisper, her hands pressed against his chest.

He kissed the soft spot under her ear. "They expect us to disappear and make use of an empty room. Wrap your arms around my neck and act like you're into it."

"I don't like this kind of audience," she objected.

"Me either, baby," he promised, kissing her neck. "But you still smell like heaven and I won't find it hard to be convincingly into you." He laced his fingers into her hair and pulled her mouth to his. "Try to do the same." His mouth closed over hers and she whimpered into his mouth.

"Hey," a guard said. "Rooms are upstairs."

Luke glanced up at him and drew Julie's hand in his. "Just warming up." He tugged Julie forward, confident anyone who missed them would be told they were getting the nasty on.

Luke glanced over his shoulder, making sure they weren't being watched, and bypassed the stairs, following the rich, spiced scent of cigars he'd smelled when he'd been near Arel. It ended at a closed door he shoved open and prayed the room beyond was empty. They entered an office, where a low burning fire was giving its last breath in a massive white hearth, giving an orange glow to the room. Silently, he was thankful for the light it expelled.

His eyes scanned the room, resting on a large desk set against one wall. Pulling Julie behind him, determined to keep her near, he moved across the room, his eyes quickly adjusting to the dim light. Once they were behind the desk, Luke settled his hands on Julie's waist and set her on top, making sure they had a cover if they were interrupted.

Luke bent down and flipped his heel open, removing the extra mic he had inside and sliding it under the desktop. He'd barely attached it, when the door jerked open behind Julie.

Luke moved instinctively, stepping towards her, pushing her legs apart as he insinuated his body between her thighs. "Wrap your legs around my waist," he whispered.

Even as she did as he said, he buried one hand in her hair, the other around her neck, and covered her mouth with his.

The door squeaked.

Footsteps echoed.

Luke broke the kiss without releasing Julie. He looked over her shoulder into Michael's suspicious eyes. "Buzz off," Luke ordered.

"You can't do this in here," he said sharply.

Luke's laugh mocked him. "If she's willing, I assure you I can."

Julie let her legs fall from his waist, but he didn't release her. Instead, he bent down and nipped at her lips.

"Hey!" Michael exclaimed insolently. "I told you no!"

Luke gave him a go to hell look. "Arel told me I could grab a room, man. Back off!"

"Upstairs. Not here. You must leave, now."

Luke scowled at the man, and then looked down at Julie. "Let's go, darlin." He moved his hands to her waist and lifted her off the desk.

Pulling her under his arm, he said, "We're out of here. Where do we go to get a ride?"

Michael's eyes narrowed as he studied Luke curiously. "There are rooms upstairs."

"Yeah, well," he said, sliding his hand around Julie's waist, "she's the only hospitality I need the rest of tonight, and I don't want to miss the last ferry off Fantasy Island here because I forgot the time."

Michael considered them a moment, and said, "Follow me." He unhooked a walkie-talkie from his belt and called for a car.

A few minutes later, he and Julie were seated in the back seat of the same car they had arrived in. Luke was certain, compliments of Blake, the car now had a tracking device attached to its belly. If the car took a turn away from the ferry, he'd have men to back him up. He didn't try to play the game of seducing Julie in the car this time. She seemed to relax next to him, as if she felt like it was over. What she didn't know, and he did, was that if they were going to be taken out, it would be now.

Chapter Twenty-Three

Luke didn't breathe again until he and Julie were out of the car at the ferry station. He took her hand and led her to the main building. He could feel relief shifting inside him, turning into something darker that had been beneath the surface since the moment he'd found Julie on the ferry.

"What happened back there with Arel?" she asked the instant they were inside the building. "I felt so in the dark while we were there and it was killing me not to be able to ask."

"He's going to give me a chance to prove myself."

"When? How?"

"I'll get a message like I did for the party." He didn't say anything else, fighting the rising storm inside him. She could have died. She shouldn't have even been here to be at risk.

He glanced at the schedule board for the boats and then the clock and by pure luck they had a few minutes to make the next ferry. He wanted the hell off of this stinking island and he didn't ever want to return, but would probably have to.

"Let's go." He pulled her along with him.

"Luke?" she asked. "What's wrong?"

"What's wrong? You could have been killed back there."

"But I wasn't."

"And Jesse better thank the good Lord above for that."

"It's not his fault, Luke. He's a great guy. I used that against him and I hated doing it, but I had to do this."

He ground his teeth, biting back some choice words about Jesse. "This isn't the time or the place," he said, and made sure she couldn't argue, he ducked a shoulder between the bodies and inched them into the center of the herd boarding the boat.

Finally, they cleared the ramp and were on the boat, the cold wind gusting around them, and people spread out all directions, trying to find their perfect travel location. Luke made a beeline for the warmer cabins.

Julie grabbed his arm, halting their progress. "Luke—"

"Not here," he said, still holding her hand. "Not now, when I'm this close to the edge. You won't like what I have to say."

She inhaled, pink spreading over her cheeks, her hair lifting off her neck in the wind. "Don't blame Jesse for this. I tricked him."

"Yeah well, he's supposed to be better than that," he said. "If he's smart he's already headed to the unemployment line."

"This is insane. You're blaming him for something I did."

"I'm making him take responsibility for something that could have gotten you killed, and if you think Royce would feel differently if this was Lauren, you're wrong."

"If you wouldn't have tried to make this decision for me, and ran off playing super hero, determined to get yourself killed then I wouldn't have done this at all. I did the right thing, and I was trying to save innocent lives. And you. I was trying to save you."

"I don't need you to save me."

"I don't need you to save me either."

"Yeah, well tough. You don't get to make that decision." A flash of that female guard searching her ripped through him. "I told you. If I have to throw you over my shoulder and carry you to some cave to protect you, I'll do it." He knew he was being dominant, even an ass, but the things that could have gone wrong back there were eating him alive.

"You have no right to do that. This is my life and my choice."

He felt those words like a knife shredding his heart. "Right. Your life, and my role is just bodyguard and good time buddy. I guess we're moving up. I used to only be the good time buddy."

She sucked in air and shook her head. "No. That's not true. You took what I said wrong."

His cell phone buzzed with a text. "Blake is on the boat. He wants us to come to him in case we're being watched."

"I guess this fight doesn't help our cover either. You were right. This isn't the place for this." Without another word, she turned and started walking. The conversation was over. Maybe they were over.

***

Ten minutes later, Luke stood on one side of the cabin with Blake, while Julie stood on the other, staring out of the sealed window.

Blake listened while Luke filled him in on the night's events before he glanced at Julie, "I thought I was the one so good at pissing off women. You're the cool, calm, diplomat that never gets rattled."

Luke massaged the ball of tension in his neck. "I guess you're rubbing off on me, because I'm excelling at pissing her off."

"Love hurts so good."

That got Luke's attention. "Who said anything about love?"

"You didn't have to. It's been the white elephant in the room for months every time you two cross paths. I'm just glad you both finally decided to stop avoiding it so we all can."

"And now it's like a head-on collision on a crash and burn mission."

"Three words. Make up sex."

"Three words. Too pissed off. I'm trying to save her life and she's trying to get killed." But it was more than that. So much more. Blake studied him for several long moments.

"You do know she was trying to save yours too, right?"

"It's not about her willingness to put her life on the line. I get what she did. I get that she cares about other people getting hurt because of her."

"But you don't think she cares about you?"

"It's not about caring." It was about how he'd felt when she told him he had no right to protect her, and not even really about the words spoken in anger. He got that she was pissed. He got that he was being overbearing and couldn't seem to help himself. But those words she'd shouted had hit a nerve and underlined his concern that she simply couldn't let him into her life.

Luke's cell rang and he pulled it from his belt and frowned at Royce's number, before answering with, "Why are you calling me from your honeymoon?" he asked, his eyes locking with Blake's in question. Blake shook his head, telling Luke he hadn't called him.

"What the hell is going on there?" Royce asked.

"Not a damn thing you should be concerned about. Go make love to your wife and leave me the hell alone."

"No go, brother. I'm halfway home already in an airport. Jesse called me and yes, he told me everything, and yes, he's packing his things. I didn't want him to until we could all talk, but he's insisting."

"You won't hear me argue his departure," Luke said. "And as for what's happening, since you're already on our way home, I'll be damn happy to have you here. Blake and I need backup we trust."

"Oh hell," he grumbled. "Just a second." Luke heard him talking to Lauren before he returned. "Our flight was cancelled. We won't be there until tomorrow around noon. Don't go getting killed on me or I'll dig you up and make your afterlife hell." He hung up.

"He's coming home," Blake said before Luke could say anything.

"He is, and as much as I hate interrupting him, we need him."

203

The ferry sounded a warning as they approached the dock. "I've already told Murphy I'd update him when we get to land. We don't need anyone from the task force anywhere near our place unless it's absolutely necessary. We'll be watched."

Julie headed their way and Blake pushed off the wall. "I'll leave you two lovebirds on your own." He sauntered forward and Julie stepped to Luke's side and held up his keys. "I stole your truck. It's in the parking lot."

He pocketed the keys. "We'll take a cab. I'd hate to spoil a night of surviving danger to get blown up in my own truck."

"I don't really want to get blown up in your truck either. I guess that's one thing we still agree on."

"Let's get off the boat," he said instead of what he really wanted to say, which was that they agreed on a lot of things, but he just wasn't sure they agreed on where they were going together. When she'd told him she needed him, he'd thought they did. Now, he wasn't so sure.

***

Julie slid into the cab and Luke joined her. Any relief she felt over escaping for the night alive was replaced with turmoil over Luke and Jesse.

He slid in beside her. "Jesse called Royce and he and Lauren are already in an airport on the way back."

"Oh no," she said, reaching for her purse to pull out her phone. "I have to stop them."

"Too late," he said. "They're stranded at their first stop. Their flight was cancelled. They'll be in tomorrow."

Julie felt the crush of reality. She'd dragged Luke into this mess. Destroyed Jesse's career and now her best friend's honeymoon. And there was nothing she could do to fix it.

By the time they'd completed the ride in complete silence, Julie wanted to burst through the cab door when they stopped. She needed to think. She needed to do something to make everything right. Escape was impossible. She was at Luke's apartment, and standing outside his door while he unlocked it, she tried to figure out what to say or do.

He shoved open the door and let her enter before coming in and going straight to the kitchen. She stood there, trying to decide what to do. Never before in her life had a man made her feel the way Luke did.

She followed him, still without a plan. He was leaning against the counter doing absolutely nothing. She leaned on the doorframe. "I don't know what to say."

"And therein lies the problem. I know exactly what I want to say, and where I want this to go. You don't."

"That's not true."

"Then tell me."

His expression was stony, his words cold. She told herself it was because she'd hurt him. Told herself to get past it, but he didn't seem receptive. In fact, he seemed like he'd already made up his mind that he was done. "I hate that I pulled you into this."

"Wrong answer," he said, and pushed off the counter to open the fridge. He grabbed a beer and twisted the top. "I'll be downstairs in the offices if you need me."

"It's two in the morning," she said, glancing at the time on the microwave.

"I'm not tired." He sauntered toward her and stopped in front of her, waiting for her to move. He was so close she could reach out and touch him. She wanted to, oh how she wanted to, but she didn't. She told herself to do it, to touch him and to hug him and to tell him how much he meant to her. She opened her mouth to say it, but somehow she didn't. She backed up and let him pass. She let him walk out of the apartment.

Julie stood there, barely able to breathe, thinking of how it had felt when she thought he'd let her walk away that day they'd gone to lunch. She rushed for the door and stopped dead in her tracks when she heard Luke and Blake talking. She let her head drop to the door. Now was not the time for confessions and she knew it. She had to wait until he got back.

But an hour later, she lay in the bed waiting and he didn't come back. Then another hour later. And yet another.

Chapter Twenty-Four

There was darkness, so much darkness, and she was cold. Her bones were brittle and her body ached. She stretched and tried to move, only she was trapped. She tried to roll over but she hit a wall. Panic rose inside her and she started to kick and punch until her knuckles ached and she could feel the blood oozing from them, and a wave of heat suffocated her. She screamed as flames surrounded her, as the fire burned the ice in her veins...

"Julie, honey, wake up! Julie!"

Julie blinked awake. "Lauren?" She pushed to a sitting position. "What happened?" Her gaze lifted to find Luke at the end of the bed, staring at her with an unreadable look.

"You were screaming bloody murder in your sleep."

"Nightmare again?" Luke asked softly.

She nodded. "Yes. About Elizabeth." Cici jumped on the bed and smacked Julie in the face with her tail.

"That'll wake you up," Lauren laughed.

"She's got all kinds of evil ways to wake a person up," Julie said, running her hand down Cici's back and noting the 9 a.m. time on the clock. "I thought you weren't coming in until lunchtime?"

"We went standby and got in earlier."

"I hate that you left your honeymoon like this."

"I hate that you didn't call us sooner."

"I'll leave you two to talk," Luke said.

"Luke," Julie said quickly.

He glanced back at her, arching a brow.

"I had something else to tell you last night, but Blake showed up."

He stared at her for a long, intense few moments, before he said, "I'm not going far. Not yet."

Not yet. There was an underlying meaning to that answer, she was certain. There was still hope. He left the room and Lauren lowered her voice, "Yowza, what was that?"

"I'll let you know when I figure it out."

***

Julie and Lauren talked for a good hour before Julie showered and pulled on a pair of black sweats and a red t-shirt Lauren had brought her. Sooner or later she had to go shopping – that was, if she lived through this mess.

Feeling ridiculously nervous about seeing Luke, she opened the bedroom door to find Luke, Royce, Blake, and Lauren sitting in the living room. Lauren stood up from the couch she shared with Royce and held a finger to her lips.

Julie stopped at the edge of the room, across from the leather chair Luke occupied and knew this call had to be Arel. After a few seconds, he ended the call. "It's not good. Arel wants me to deliver a certain piece of art by tonight."

"That's impossible," Blake said in disbelief.

"Tonight?" Royce asked.

"The impossibility seems to be the point. It's that or he gave me another option."

"The journal," Julie said, remembering what Luke had said when her apartment had been trashed about not underestimating Arel.

"So basically," Royce said. "He wants the journal."

"You can't give the journal to him," Julie said. "It's part of the proof you need to take down the cartel."

"We'll just have to copy it before we give it to him," Blake said. "He has to know that."

"And he probably knows that might not even be admissible in court," Lauren said, putting her criminal law degree to work, "and certainly it would leave room for speculation about tampering with documents."

"It's less damning to Arel than it is to the judge and Dragonfly," Luke said. "This is the kiss of death for them."

"How does Arel know about the journal?" Lauren asked.

"Maybe they tortured Elizabeth before they killed her," Luke said. "Maybe they tapped the sister's phone. There are too many possibilities. We need me inside this operation to take down Arel. We have to give him the journal."

"Agreed," Royce said.

"Agreed," Blake added. "So how does this go down?"

"I'll get a call and instructions," Luke said. "

"Of course," Royce said. "Giving us no time to plan."

"I'll call Hendrix and Murphy and round up the rest of our team for a planning session," Blake said, pushing to his feet.

"It should be a simple drop, shouldn't it?" Lauren asked. "It's what he wants."

"We don't ever assume anything is simple or as it seems."

***

An hour later, Luke and his brothers had Murphy and Hendrix on speakerphone, trying to get a grip on just how many people they needed to be involved tonight.

"I don't mean to be the Grim Reaper," Blake said, "but this could all be about the journal, not about trust. They get it and take Luke out. We need to be ready for this."

Luke had already thought of that. "It's a strong possibility."

"Which makes my immediate concern is that we're headed back to the island and that means moving out now," Blake said. "We need a team there yesterday."

"It could be in the city," Murphy said. "Arel does the unexpected."

"We have to be ready for both," Hendrix said.

""That will mean splitting up, which will leave Luke with less support," Royce said. "I don't like it."

"But not splitting up," Hendrix countered, "could mean he ends up with no support."

"I'm staying with Luke," Blake said and he glanced at Luke. "Jesse knows the city like his own stink, man. We need him and we need manpower."

Luke considered a moment, fighting personal feelings to focus on the reality of a grim situation. "Fine. Call him."

"I'll stay here too," Hendrix said. "I know this city pretty damn well myself. Murphy should go. One of us needs to be at both locations since we're accountable to the task force."

Royce eyed Murphy. "You, me, and my man Kyle, on the island?"

Murphy nodded. "Works for me. We still keeping the rest of the task force out of this?"

"Until we know who Dragonfly is," Luke said. "Yes."

"I say Luke wears a wire," Blake said.

Luke shook his head. "They'll pat me down. I'll have to try and record with my cell phone."

A general mumbling of approval filled the room.

"This call could come at any moment," Luke said. "So we need to get this rolling now."

Murphy ran a hand over his hair. "I just hope this really is a test. If Luke is in Arel's circle after this, then maybe we really can get answers about our missing agent and shut him down." He eyed Luke. "So don't go getting killed, how about it?"

Luke didn't plan on dying and he knew that meant keeping his head clear. If he went to his apartment, if he let himself get worked up over Julie, he wouldn't.

***

Julie spent the afternoon with Lauren, who offered her a much-needed distraction by way of honeymoon stories and pictures, especially since Luke hadn't so much as called her.

They were sitting at Luke's kitchen table, where Julie had her laptop open, trying to do a bit of work, when Lauren's cell rang. Julie listened to her talk to Royce, and watched how her friend glowed just talking to her new husband.

Lauren ended the call. "They're still working on preparation. I'm going to head out to stay with Royce on the island later."

"Okay," Julie said, rising to her feet and refilling her coffee cup, trying not to think about how badly she wanted to see Luke and talk to him.

"You want to talk about Luke?"

"Not yet," she said. "But eventually."

"That's closer to talking about him than we've ever gotten, so I'm pretty pleased with that answer. You normally shut me down when Luke comes up. Just know that I'm here when you need me."

"I know," Julie said. "And thank you."

The door to the apartment opened and shut. Luke appeared in the doorway and Lauren got up. "I need to go unpack." She hugged Julie. "I'll be back in a bit."

Julie and Luke stared at each other. The door opened and closed again. They were alone. "I had to go last night. I didn't want to lose you. Luke, I–" She set her cup down and ran to him, throwing her arms around him. He didn't hold her, didn't touch her, but she wasn't going to back down. "I don't want to lose you. Don't shut me out because you think I meant something I didn't. I'm not used to feeling like this. You're not just some 'bedroom buddy'. I don't know how to prove that–"

He kissed her, oh god how he kissed her. Hot, passionate, deliciously possessive. She lifted to her toes, trying to get more of him, trying to show him how much she needed him.

He tore his mouth from hers, tangled his hand in her hair and stared down at her. "I'm going to protect you at all costs."

"I know."

"You won't always like it."

"I know that, too, but you have to accept I'll do the same for you."

He kissed her again and lifted her to the counter, sliding her legs apart to press his hips between them, bringing his mouth just above hers, before his lips curved. "I'm not your bedroom buddy?"

She smiled at the term 'bedroom buddy' he'd pulled from some random hat. "Sure you don't want to reconsider that?"

The door opened and closed and Blake called out, "Luke!"

Luke pressed his forehead to Julie's. "Leave it to my brother to have crap timing."

Blake walked into the kitchen. "Oh hey, you two. Glad to see you made up." He sat down at the table. "I got the map of the city to review with you, Luke."

Luke made an exasperated sound. "We'll continue this later," he said to Julie and set her on the ground.

"Anyone else hungry?"

Luke gave her a look that said 'yes.' He was hungry for her. And for the first time ever, a lustful look in a man's eyes made her heart skip a beat.

***

It was nearly eleven o'clock and Julie paced the small space in front of Luke's fireplace while he and Blake watched. Luke patted his chair. "Will you please come sit down? You're wearing a hole in the floor."

Blake motioned to the television. "ESPN is on. You love sports."

"When are they going to call?" she asked.

"They'll call," Luke said and his cell phone rang. "See?"

Blake stood up and crossed his arms in front of his chest, ready for action. Luke punched the button and listened and then hung up.

"Well?" the entire room asked at once.

"Subway car number nine at midnight."

"Shit," Blake blurted and started to pace in the very same area Julie had just been doing the same. "Shit, shit, shit, shit." He dialed Royce and gave him the news. He ended the call and gave them a quick update. "Hendrix and Jesse are on his way up from the street. I'm going to meet them at the side door so he won't be seen. I'm sure you both know this, but the tunnels will make surveillance impossible. We need to talk this out."

Julie's eyes met Luke's. "How bad is this setup?"

"No cell phone reception," he said. "And once I'm on the train, I'm on my own."

Julie held up the train schedule she'd been studying. "That train is an express to Queens. That means no stops for at least fifteen minutes."

"But you can take a gun, right? They can't check you closely in the middle of the subway."

"Unless they've found a way around that."

"We're here," Blake said, hurrying back into the room with Hendrix by his side.

"That train is an express to Queens," Jesse said.

"We just figured that out," Luke said.

"So someone needs to be on the train when it arrives. Someone they won't recognize."

"They don't know me," Hendrix said, sitting down on the couch. "I'll do it. I'll head there now."

"I'll go with him," Jesse chimed in.

"I'll tail Luke in case they try to get to him before he gets to the subway," Blake said and glanced at Luke. "I'll go get a uniform of guns and knives on, and meet you in the garage in five minutes?"

Luke gave a nod. "That works." His attention went to Julie and when Blake exited the apartment, she darted towards him and hugged him.

"I have a really bad feeling about this," she said. "Don't you dare get killed, you hear me?"

"Sweetheart," he said, softly. "I'm not going anywhere. You're stuck with me, whether you like it or not."

"You better." And once again, she found herself thinking that she'd only just found Luke again. She couldn't lose him.

Chapter Twenty-Five

Julie sat in the kitchen of Luke's apartment finishing off a pint of ice cream from his freezer because what else did a girl do when worried senseless but eat ice cream? But now it was gone, and she was still a wreck, so she thought the only other logical thing to do was to go back to her pacing in front of the fireplace.

She tossed the empty pint and was headed that way when she heard what sounded like the ring tone for Blake's cell. Sure enough, there it was. She frowned. This was so not like him, and so not well timed.

She grabbed the phone and answered, afraid someone on the team was looking for him. Immediately, a man with a heavy French accent said, "Call me the minute you have the journal. Do not fail me, or you will be a dead Dragonfly."

The line went dead. She looked at the phone and flipped through the numbers. It wasn't Blake's phone at all. It belonged to Hendrix.

Julie couldn't breathe. Her hand went to her chest. She dialed Blake. No answer. She dialed Luke. No answer. She dialed Jesse. No answer. They were all in the tunnels. Finally, Royce answered. "Hendrix is Dragonfly. I can't reach anyone to tell them." She quickly told him what happened.

"Keep trying to call them," he said, "and I will too. I'm stuck on the ferry."

Julie hung up and kept dialing over and over. No answer from anyone. She had to warn Luke. She ran for her purse and headed for the door.

***

The Flamingo Hotel was yet another dingy dive of a place that fed drugs, prostitution, and other sordid habits. Alone in the room she was given, Gina sat on the edge of a bumpy bed with an ugly orange bedspread, pondered how well Marco knew the people at the front desk. They had treated him as if he was their boss or something.

Gina wasn't sure what it was about Marco that made her want to please him so, but she did. Perhaps it was simply his exceptional body and phenomenal skill as a lover.

Then again, there was a distinct possibility it was their mutual love of money that intrigued her. The ruthless way his mind worked was downright evil, giving him a dangerously alluring air that clung to him like a well fitted suit.

It was downright sexy.

Tonight's agenda was brilliant. She'd told the judge she didn't have the journal so she'd make it up to him until she did. She couldn't wait to see the judge's face when ... A knock sounded on the door, drawing her attention.

"Time for the show," she whispered with anticipation dancing through every fiber of her body.

Stopping at the broken mirror that sat on top of the scuffed white dresser, she smiled at her image. Dressed in a fire engine red lingerie set complete with garters, a tiny lacy bra, barely-there panties, and spiked heels, she was deliciously ready for action.

The knock on the door sounded again. "Anxious," she said with one last look in the mirror as a devilish smile tilted up her painted red lips.

Sashaying to the door she opened it and leaned on the wall in a sexy come-hither way that displayed her body. "Evening, Judge."

Judge Moore gave her a heavy-lidded, slow perusal. When he was finished, he stepped forward, wrapping his arms around her as he maneuvered them both into the room and pushed the door shut.

"You look good enough to eat," he said as he spread his hands around the bare cheeks of her backside and pressed her against the hardness of his body.

"Slow down, baby. Tonight, we're going to play a little game." She pushed out of his arms.

The judge started unbuttoning his shirt. "I like games."

"Good," Gina said smiling seductively. "You have to promise to follow my rules. Tonight, I'm in charge." Gina walked up to him and pressed her palm against his bulging zipper. "You'll be rewarded for good behavior."

The judge covered her hand with his own making her press harder. Gina tsked. "Not yet, Judge. I won't play at all if you don't obey."

He stared at her as if deciding how serious she was, and then reluctantly released her hand. Gina stepped back and leaned on the dresser. "Get naked. I want to watch."

"If I do, what do I get in return?"

Her eyes narrowed, her voice hardened. "No questions, no demands. I'm in charge. Want to play or not?" The words were like the flick of a whip.

There was a long silence before the judge shoved his shirt to the ground, and then quickly toed off his shoes before stripping off the remainder of his clothes. Standing before her naked and erect, he smiled.

Gina walked toward him, stopping a mere inch from touching him. She looked him up and down, and then circled him. When she was behind him she smacked his backside. Hard.

He started to turn. "Hey."

She pressed her fingers in his back. "My rules," she warned. When he turned again she smacked him even harder. He didn't turn this time. "Lie on the bed."

When he was flat on his back Gina opened a dresser drawer and pulled out three scarves. His eyes widened but he didn't say anything. Standing above him she let one of the scarves lightly trail around his erection. He jerked slightly, his eyes closing.

She picked up one of his hands and he reached for her with the other. She pointed at his hand. "Stop, or else." He did. Seconds later both of his hands were tied. She straddled him, intentionally teasing him as she blindfolded him.

Leaning down, pressing her chest against his, her bottom against his erection, she whispered in his ear. "How's it feel being helpless, Judge?"

He moaned. "Like I'm going to go crazy if you don't touch me soon."

Laughing softly, Gina moved off him. "Come back," he said urgently.

"Soon," she said as she moved towards the door. She pulled it open and smiled at Marco.

His brow inched up. "It is done?"

One side of her mouth inched up. "Of course."

"Excellent." Gina stepped back to allow him to enter. Once in the room he walked to the judge and tightened the knots on his wrists.

"Who's there?" the judge said abruptly. "Gina?"

"Gina is here," Marco said and watched the judge stiffen.

Even with the blindfold, his features showed fear. Though Marco had never met the judge, his French accent was an easy giveaway of his relationship to Arel.

"What in the hell?" the judge blurted out. He started to tug on the restraints.

"Calm down," Gina told him. "It's just a little game."

The judge didn't listen, bucking with panic.

"Enough!" Marco blurted and yanked a gun from his waistband. He pressed it to the judge's temple and cocked it. "Be still or I will shoot."

The judge froze.

"You are going to have a good time, Judge," Marco assured him with absolute truth in his words. "You and Gina are going to play. I like to watch, it's really quite simple. As long as you do as you are told, it will be painless." He paused and let the words sink in. "Understood?"

Slowly the judge nodded.

"Good," Marco said and set the gun on the end table. "Get a glass of water, and come here, Gina."

Gina did as he instructed and then sashayed over to Marco, setting the glass on the table and pressing her body against his. "Can I warm up on you, baby?" she asked as her hand explored the ripples of muscle she loved along his shoulders.

"Non," he said. "I'll watch." He pressed a strip of sweetness to her lips and she swallowed it. He gave her another. "More. Tonight is special."

Marco handed her four strips. "Give them to him."

She sashayed over to him and ripped off the blindfold. She wanted to see the panic in his eyes.

"Forget it," The judge bit out through clenched teeth. "I'm not taking that."

Marco picked up the gun and held it to his head again. "The drugs will make you feel good. The gun, I assure you, will not."

The judge took the drugs.

Chapter Twenty-Six

Luke reached the stairs, his coat concealing a variety of weapons and the journal. He might have to get rid of most of them, but he was banking on keeping at least one. He headed through the entry gates and then down the stairs to the train terminal where there were nothing but concrete beams and benches.

Footsteps sounded behind him and he turned to find Hendrix coming down the stairs with a gun in his hand and with three other men following him. "Move to the concrete pole and put your hands on it."

"You're Dragonfly," Luke said. "I should have known."

"Should have, would have, could have," he said. "But you didn't and I can shoot you and get away with it, so I suggest you move."

Luke pressed his hands to the concrete wall, and two men came to stand on either side of him. One searched him and handed off his four guns and two knives, before grabbing the journal.

The men backed away and Luke turned to watch Hendrix set the journal on fire and then throw it onto the tracks. "That was easy," he said brushing his hands together. "I thought you Walker brothers were good?" He shrugged. "Guess not."

"Was it the money that turned you, or were you always like this?" Luke asked.

"Money, power, more money. It makes the world go round."

"The missing agent—"

"She got too close. Hell, she was sharper than you Walkers. She had to be dealt with. Just like you."

"And my brothers?"

"Will never know I was involved."

"Ouch," a familiar voice said. "Don't pull so hard."

Luke's blood ran cold at the sound of Julie's voice. She appeared on the stairs, being pulled forward by another one of Hendrix's men.

"Look what we have here," Hendrix said as she was shoved toward him. "Nice taste, by the way," he said looking her up and down and flicking a taunting glance at Luke. "Perhaps I can sample the goods before we do away with her."

She didn't react, as if she knew it would please him. Her eyes met Luke's. "I figured out it was him, and I tried to warn you."

"Better late to the party than never," Hendrix said and winked. He walked towards her, stopped directly beside her. "You certainly will liven up this little party. How should we get started?"

"Touch her and you die," Luke promised, his voice low, lethal. "You're dead anyway, Hendrix."

Hendrix gave an exaggerated laugh. "I hardly think you're in a position to be making threats." He looked at his watch. "The next train will be here in five minutes." He called over his shoulder. "Pull the car to the exit."

"Luke," Julie said. "There's something I should have told you and I didn't."

"Shut up!" Hendrix said, and cut a look to the man holding her. "Deal with her."

The man slapped her. Julie yelped with the pain, and pressed her hand to her cheek.

Hendrix smirked at Luke. "Come and get me." He pointed to a guard. "Tell Marco the journal was destroyed before we could get to it. Make it convincing."

"All this so you don't get in trouble with Arel over that damn journal," Luke said. "You really are a sick man."

Hendrix laughed. "I am what I am, and that's smarter than you."

The wind picked up as faint sounds of the approaching train humming through the tunnel. "Let's go," Hendrix said to the men, and moved towards the stairs.

One of the men holding guns on Luke motioned for him to move forward. Hendrix and two other men were already headed up the stairs. The odds just improved. That left Luke with his guard and Julie's to dispose of. The trick was making sure Julie was safe.

The subway car was approaching. Luke's guard shifted his eyes toward it, and gave Luke the opportunity. He grabbed the man, covered his gun hand with his own, and fired on the other guard. Before he ever hit the ground, Luke had turned, taken the gun fully from the man he still held and put a bullet in him, too.

Luke pointed the gun, surveying the area for anyone else. "Grab the other gun," he ordered Julie, "and if in doubt, use it."

The subway car came to a stop and Luke rotated around to point his weapon. Jesse came out, his gun raised, and fired at the stairs. A man rolled down the steps, his gun falling to the pavement.

"That's close to even," Luke said. "But you aren't there yet."

"Close is better than nothing," Jesse said, joining Luke. "Where's Hendrix? He disappeared on me."

"He's Dragonfly," Julie said, "and how do we get out of here?"

"Everyone okay down there?" Royce shouted from above.

"All clear," Luke shouted.

"Batman has arrived," Blake said, appearing on the stairs, two guns in his hand. "Hendrix is dead. Three others in custody. Two others escaped."

Royce followed Blake down the stairs. "How is it you lost your phone again?"

"We have the same phone, brother dearest. He grabbed mine. And in case you didn't notice, that's what warned us about Hendrix before it was too late." Sirens screamed above ground. "The cavalry has arrived."

Luke went over to Julie, who was staring at the dead bodies, the gun still in her hand. "You okay?" he asked, removing the gun from her hand.

She nodded, lifted her gaze to his. "I love you."

"What?" he asked, shocked by the sudden confession.

"I love you and I should have told you before now, and I don't want to risk ending up like them and you never knowing. I love you."

He shoved the gun into his coat and wrapped his arms around her. "I love you, too."

She blinked. "You do?"

"Yes. I do."

Murphy rushed down the stairs. "Arel's house is cleared out and we just got a call from a motel a few blocks away. The judge and Julie's secretary were found dead."

Blake scrubbed his jaw. "You really know how to mess up a romance novel moment, man."

Chapter Twenty-Seven

Julie was exhausted by early morning when she, Luke, and his brothers returned to the Walker apartment. The questions had been many, the answers not as easily found as everyone wanted. The missing agent was most likely dead. Gina and the judge were dead. Arel had disappeared along with every known operation he'd been involved with that the task force had known about.

Julie looked around Luke's kitchen, eying Luke's brothers and Lauren, with an odd feeling of belonging she'd never before experienced. She sat on Luke's lap, as Lauren did Royce's. Blake, as usual, was eating, stuffing his third donut in his mouth. To watch them together made her experience a little part of something warm and wonderful that she had never known. To be with them helped make the night's tragedy just a little more bearable.

"Have a donut," Blake said to Julie pushing the box in her direction.

"I'm too tired to eat," she said.

"I'm never too tired to eat," Blake commented, and the room broke into laughter.

"Yes, we know," Julie said smiling.

Blake finished off his donut and stood up. "Time for beddy-bye."

"Us too," Royce said and Lauren climbed off his lap.

"I know you're tired," Lauren said to Julie, "but tomorrow let's talk about you leaving divorce behind and coming to work with my new firm."

"Yes," Julie said. "I'd like that." She was ready to leave the past behind, ready to take some risks.

Goodbyes were said, and soon Julie was alone with Luke. She had no idea what had gotten into her, but now that she'd taken the step to confess her love for Luke, she was feeling daring all over again.

"Luke," she said, caressing his cheek. "Will you marry me?"

Luke stared at her, a stunned look on his face before his lips curved into a smile. "You know you just stole my thunder, right?"

"What do you mean?"

"Us macho Walker men like to go down on one knee and propose properly. And I'm supposed to have the ring first."

"Oh, right," she said, smiling at his response. "So, now what do we do?"

He set her on her feet and then back in the chair and went down on one knee. "Julie. Will you marry me?"

She laughed and wrapped her arms around his neck, feeling like she was home for the first time in her life.

Please visit my website for excerpts and monthly contests! I give away a gift card every month to a reader.

www.lisareneejones.com

And now a look at IF I WERE YOU....
Book 1 of THE INSIDE OUT SERIES
OPTIONED TO STARZ for cable TV with
Suzanne Todd(Alice in Wonderland w/Johnny Depp)
producing.

Excerpt:

We begin our walk, faster this time, and the cold wind has nothing on the chill between us. Conversation is non-existent, and I have no clue how to break the silence, or if I should even try. I dare a peek at his profile several times, fighting the wind blowing hair over my eyes, but he doesn't acknowledge me. Why won't he look at me? Several times, I open my mouth to speak but words simply won't leave my lips.

We are almost to the gallery, and a knot has formed in my stomach at the prospect of an awkward goodbye, when he suddenly grabs me and pulls me into a small enclave of a deserted office rental. Before I can fully grasp what is happening, I am against the wall, hidden from the street and he is in front of me, enclosing me in the tiny space. I blink up into his burning stare and I think I might combust. His scent, his warmth, his hard body, is all around me, but he is not touching me. I *want* him to touch me.

He presses his hand to the concrete wall above my head when I want it on my body. "You don't belong here, Sara."

The words are unexpected, a hard punch in the chest. "What? I don't understand."

"This job is wrong for you."

I shake my head. I don't belong? Coming from Chris, an established artist, I feel inferior, rejected. "You asked me why I wasn't following my heart. Why I wasn't pursuing what I love. I am. That's what I'm doing."

"I didn't think you'd do it in this place."

This place. I don't know what he's telling me. Does he mean this gallery? This city? Has he judged me not worthy of his inner circle?

"Look, Sara." He hesitates, and lifts his head to the sky, seeming to struggle for words before fixing me with a turbulent look. "I'm trying to protect you here. This world you've strayed into is filled with dark, messed up, arrogant assholes who will play with your mind and use you until there is nothing else left for you to recognize in yourself."

"Are you one of those dark, messed up, arrogant assholes?"

He stares down at me, and I barely recognize the hard lines of his face, the glint in his eyes, as belonging to the man I've just had lunch with. His gaze sweeps my lips, lingers, and the swell of response and longing in me is instant, overwhelming. He reaches up and strokes his thumb over my bottom lip. Every nerve ending in my body responds and it's all I can do not to touch him, to grab his hand, but something holds me back. I am lost in this man, in his stare, in some spellbinding, dark whirlwind of…what? Lust, desire, torment? Seconds tick eternally and so does the silence. I want to hold him, to stop whatever I sense is coming but I cannot.

"I'm worse." He pushes off the wall, and is gone. He is gone. I am alone against the wall, aching with a fire that has nothing to do with the meal we shared. My lashes flutter, my fingers touch my lip where he touched me. He has warned me away from Mark, from the gallery, from him, and he has failed. I cannot turn away. I am here and I am going nowhere.

Buy it on Amazon.com
Visit Lisa for updates on the show here:

www.lisareneejones.com

Made in the USA
Lexington, KY
10 March 2015